Susan Carlisle's love affair with books began in the sixth grade, when she made a bad grade in mathematics. Not allowed to watch TV until she'd brought the grade up, Susan filled her time with books. She turned her love of reading into a passion for writing, and now has over ten Medical Romances published through Mills & Boon. She writes about hot, sexy docs and the strong women who captivate them. Visit SusanCarlisle.com.

FIREFIGHTER'S UNEXPECTED FLING

SUSAN CARLISLE

MILLS & BOON

First published in Great Britain 2019
by Mills & Boon, an imprint of HarperCollins*Publishers*
1 London Bridge Street, London, SE1 9GF

Large Print edition 2020

© 2019 Susan Carlisle

ISBN: 978-0-263-08570-9

This book is produced from independently certified
FSC™ paper to ensure responsible forest management. For
more information visit www.harpercollins.co.uk/green.

Printed and bound in Great Britain
by CPI Group (UK) Ltd, Croydon, CR0 4YY

To Brandon Ray
Some family you love even though
they married in!

CHAPTER ONE

SALLY DAVIS PULLED her bag and a portable bottle of oxygen out of the back of the ambulance. The heat from the burning abandoned warehouse was almost unbearable. Her work coveralls were sticking to her sweating body.

This structural fire was the worst she'd seen as a paramedic working with the Austin, Texas, Fire Department over the last year. Her heart had leaped as the adrenaline had started pumping when the call had woken her and the dispatcher had announced what was involved. These were the fires she feared the most. With a warehouse like this, there was no telling who or what was inside. There were just too many opportunities for injury, or worse.

She watched as the flames grew. The popping and cracking of the building burning was an ironic contrast to the peace of the sun rising on the horizon. She didn't have time to appreciate it though. She had a job to do.

Moments later a voice yelled, "There's someone in there!"

Sally's mouth dropped open in shock as she saw Captain Ross Lawson run into the flames. Even in full turnout gear with the faceplate of his helmet pulled down and oxygen tank on his back, she recognized his tall form and broad shoulders. Sally's breath caught in her chest. What was wrong with him? Her heartbeat drummed in her ears as she searched the doorway, hoping…

Sally had seen firefighters enter a burning building before but never one as completely enveloped as this one. She gripped the handle of her supply box. Would Ross make it out? Would there be someone with him?

The firefighters manning the hoses focused the water on the door, pushing back the blaze.

Every muscle in her body tightened as the tension and anticipation grew. Ross was more of an acquaintance, as she'd only shared a few shifts with him since moving to Austin. However, he and her brother were good friends. More than once she'd heard Kody praise Ross. From what little she knew about him he deserved Kody's admiration.

Right now, in this moment, as she waited with fear starting to strangle her, she questioned Ross's decision-making. Since she had joined the volunteer fire department back in North Carolina, Sally had been taught that judgment calls were *always* based on the safety of the firefighter. She doubted Ross had even given his welfare any thought before rushing into the fire.

The loss of one life would be terrible enough but the loss of a second trying to save the first wasn't acceptable. In her opinion, Ross was taking too great a risk, the danger too high. He hadn't struck her as a daredevil or adrenaline junkie but, then again, she didn't know him that well. Was this particular characteristic of Captain Lawson's one of the reasons Kody thought so highly of him?

James, the emergency medical tech working with her, stepped next to her. "That takes guts."

A form appeared in the doorway, then burst out carrying a man across his shoulders. The sixty pounds of fire equipment he wore in addition to the man's weight meant Ross was carrying more than his own body weight. Sally had to respect his physical stamina, if not his reckless determination.

Two firefighters rushed to help him, but he fell to the ground before they could catch him. The man he carried rolled off his back to lie unmoving beside him, smoke smoldering from his clothes.

"You take Captain Lawson. I'll see to the man," Sally said to James as she ran to them.

Ross jerked off his helmet and came up on his hands and knees, coughing.

Placing the portable oxygen tank on the ground, she went to her knees beside the rescued man, clearly homeless and using the warehouse to sleep in, and leaned over, putting her cheek close to his mouth. As the senior paramedic at the scene, she needed to check the more seriously injured person. Ross had been using oxygen while the homeless man had not.

Her patient was breathing, barely. She quickly positioned the face mask over his mouth and nose, then turned the valve on the tank so that two liters of oxygen flowed. By rote she found and checked his pulse. Next, she searched for any injuries, especially burns. She located a couple on his hands and face. Using the radio, she called all the information in to the hospital.

"We need to get this man transported STAT," Sally called to her partner.

Another ambulance had arrived and took over the care of Ross, leaving James free to pull a gurney her way. With the efficiency of years of practice, they loaded the man and started toward the ambulance. She called to the EMT now taking care of Ross. "How's he doing?"

The EMT didn't take his eyes off Ross as he said, "He's taken in a lot of smoke but otherwise he's good."

"Get him in a box. I still want him seen," she ordered.

Ross shook his head. "I'm fine." He coughed several times.

"I'm the medic in charge. You're going to the hospital to be checked out, Captain."

He went into another coughing fit as she hurried away. She left the EMT to see that the stubborn captain was transported back to the hospital.

Minutes later she was in the back of the ambulance—the box, as it was affectionately known—with the homeless man. While they moved at a rapid speed, she kept busy checking his vitals and relaying to the hospital emergency room the latest stats. The staff would be prepared for the patient's arrival.

The ambulance pulled to a stop and moments later the back doors were opened. They had arrived at the hospital. A couple of the staff had been waiting outside for them. Sally and one of the techs removed the gurney with the man on it.

As other medical personnel began hooking him up to monitors, she reported quickly to the young staff nurse, "This is a John Doe for now. He was in a burning warehouse. Acute smoke inhalation is the place to start."

Just as she was finishing up her report, the gurney with Ross went by. She followed it into the examination room next to the John Doe. Ross's coat had been removed and his T-shirt pulled up. He still wore his yellow firefighter pants that were blackened in places. Square stickers with monitoring wires had been placed on his chest connecting him to machines nearby. Aware of how inappropriate it was for her to admire the contours of his well-defined chest and abdomen, she couldn't stop herself.

The man kept himself in top physical shape. It was necessary with his field of work but his physique suggested he strove to surpass the norm. No wonder he'd been able to carry the man out of the burning building.

His gaze met hers. Heated embarrassment washed over her and she averted her eyes. Ogling a man, especially one that she worked with, wasn't what she should be doing.

Ross went into another round of heavy coughing that sent her attention to the amount of oxygen he was receiving. The bubble in the meter indicated one liter, which was good. Still, at this rate it would take him days to clear the smoke from his lungs.

Sally stepped closer to his side and spoke to no one in particular. "How's he doing?"

One of the nurses responded. "He seems to be recovering well. We're going to continue to give him oxygen and get a chest X-ray just to be sure that he didn't inhale any more smoke than we anticipated."

"I'm right here, you know." Ross's voice was a rusty muffled sound beneath the mask. He glared at her. This time her look remained on him.

"You need to save your voice."

He grimaced as a doctor entered. What was that look about? Surely, he wasn't afraid of doctors.

Slipping out of the room as the woman started her examination, Sally stepped to the department desk and signed papers releasing Ross and the John Doe as her patients into the hospital's care. Done, she joined the EMTs at her ambulance.

She gave James a wry smile. "Good work out there this morning."

"You too," he replied as he pulled out of the drive.

In the passenger seat, she buckled up, glad to be out of the back of the box. She wasn't a big fan of riding there.

She shivered now at the memory of when she'd been locked in a trunk and forgotten while playing a childhood game. To this day she didn't like tight spaces or the dark. Being in the square box of the ambulance reminded her too much of that experience. It was one of those things she just dealt with because she loved her job.

Sally leaned her head back and closed her

eyes. Ross's light blue gaze over the oxygen mask came to mind. She'd met Ross Lawson soon after she had moved to Austin and gone to work for the Austin Medical Emergency Service, the medical service arm that worked in conjunction with the fire department that shared the same stations and sometimes the same personnel when a fireman was also qualified to work the medical side. As an advanced paramedic, she was assigned Station Twelve, one of the busiest houses of Austin's forty-eight stations. It just happened that it was the same station where her brother and Ross worked. She hadn't missed that twinge of attraction when she and Ross had first met any more than she had this morning. But she had never acted on it and never would.

A relationship, of any kind, was no longer a priority for her. She'd had that. Her brief marriage had been both sad and disappointing. Now she was no longer married, all she wanted to do was focus on getting into medical school. It had been her dream before she'd married, and it was still her dream. At this point in her life a relationship would just be a distraction, even if she wanted one. She was done making concessions for a man. Going after what she wanted was what mattered.

The ambulance reversed with a beep, beep, beep. It alerted her to the fact that they had arrived at the firehouse. When they stopped, she hopped out onto the spotless floor.

She loved the look of the fire station. It was a modern version of the old traditional fire halls with its redbrick exterior and high arched glass doors. A ceramic dalmatian dog even sat next to the main entrance. The firefighters worked on one side of the building and the emergency crew on the other. They shared a kitchen, workout room and TV room on the firefighter side. They were a station family.

James had backed into the bay closest to the medical side of the building. The other two bays were for the engine, quint truck and rescue truck. They hadn't returned yet. The company would still be at the warehouse fire mopping up. When they did return, they would also pull in backward, ready for the next run.

Before she could even think about cleaning up and heading home, she would have to restock the ambulance and write a report. The ambulance must always be ready to roll out.

More than once in the last year she'd returned from a call only to turn around and make another one.

"Hey, Sweet Pea."

She groaned and turned to see Kody loping toward her. "I told you not to call me that," she whispered. "Especially not here."

He gave her a contrite look. "Sorry, I forgot."

"What're you doing here anyway?"

"I left something in my locker and had to stop by and get it. My shift isn't until tomorrow."

Sally smiled. She couldn't help but be glad to see her older brother. Even if it was for a few minutes. He was a good one and she had no doubt he loved her. Sometimes too much. He tended toward being overprotective. But when she'd needed to reinvent her life, Kody had been there to help. She would always be grateful.

"I heard that Ross was the hero of the day this morning." He sounded excited.

"Yeah, you could say that." He'd scared the fool out of her.

"You don't think so?"

Sally started toward the supply room. "He could have been killed."

Kody's voice softened. "He knows what he's doing. I don't know of a better firefighter."

"He ran into a fully enveloped burning warehouse!" Sally was surprised how her voice rose and held so much emotion.

"I'm sure you've seen worse. Why're you so upset?"

"I'm not upset. It just seemed overly dangerous to me. Instead of one person being hurt there, for a moment I thought it was going to be two. He has a bad case of smoke inhalation as it is." She pulled a couple of oxygen masks off a shelf.

"How's he doing?" Kody had real concern in his voice.

She looked for another piece of plastic line. "He's at the hospital but he should be released soon. They were running a few more tests when I left."

"He's bucking for a promotion, so I guess this'll look good on his résumé. See you later."

"Bye." She headed back to the ambulance with her arms full. She had no interest in Ross's ambitions and yet, for some reason, his heroics had been particularly difficult for her to watch.

* * *

Ross returned to the station a week after the warehouse fire. He had missed two shifts. The doctor had insisted, despite his arguments. He liked having time to work on his ranch but the interviews for one of the eight Battalion Chief positions were coming up soon and he should be at the station in case there were important visitors. Now that he was back, he needed to concentrate on what was ahead, what he'd planned to do since he was a boy.

Thankfully the man he'd gone in after was doing okay. He would have a stay in the burn unit but would recover. Just as Ross and his grandfather had. Ross rolled his shoulder, remembering the years' old pain.

He'd hated to miss all that time at the station, but it had taken more time to clear his lungs than he had expected. Still, he had saved that man's life. He didn't advocate running into fully engulfed houses, but memories of that horrible night when he was young had compelled him into action before he'd known what he was doing.

Memories of that night washed over him. He'd been visiting his grandpa, who'd lived in a small clapboard house outside of town. He'd adored the old man, thought he could do no wrong. His grandfather had taught Ross how to work with his hands. Shown him how to mend a fence, handle a horse. Most of what he knew he'd learned at his grandfather's side. His parents had been too busy with their lives to care. So most weekends and holidays between the ages of ten and fourteen Ross could be found at his grandfather's small ranch.

The night of the fire, Ross had been shaken awake by his grandpa. Ross could still hear his gruff smoke-filled voice. "Boy, the place is on fire. Get down and crawl to the front door. I'll be behind you."

The smoke had burned Ross's throat and eyes, but he'd done as he was told. He'd remembered what the firefighter who had come to his school had said: "Stop, drop and roll." Ross had scrambled to the door but not before a piece of burning wood had fallen on his shoulder. But the pain hadn't overridden his horror. He'd wanted out of the house. Had been glad for the fresh air. He'd run across the lawn. It had been too hot close to the house. Ross had coughed and coughed, just as he had the other morning, seeming never to draw in a full deep breath. He'd looked back for his grandpa but hadn't seen him. The fear had threatened to swallow him. His eyes had watered more from tears than smoke.

Someone must've seen the flames because the volunteer fire department had been coming up the long drive. Ross had managed between coughs and gasps of air to point and say, "My grandpa's in there."

The man hadn't hesitated before he'd run toward the house. Ross had watched in shock as he'd entered the front door. Moments later he'd come out, pulling his grandpa onto the porch and down the steps and straight toward the waiting medics. It wasn't until then that Ross had noticed the full agony of his back.

Both he and his grandpa had spent some time in the hospital. They'd had burns and lung issues. His grandfather had been told by the arson investigator that he believed the fire had started from a spark from the woodstove. Ross only knew for sure he was glad his grandpa and he had survived. Regardless of what had started the fire, Ross still carried large puckered scars on his back and shoulder as a reminder of that fateful night.

Last week, the moment he'd learned there was someone in the house he'd reacted before thinking. His Battalion Chief hadn't been pleased. Only because the outcome had been positive had Ross managed to come out without it damaging his career. He had been told in no uncertain terms that it wasn't to happen again. The message had been loud and clear: don't have any marks against you or you won't make Battalion Chief.

It was midafternoon when he was out with the rest of the company doing their daily checkup and review of the equipment that he saw Sal walking to the ambulance. Her black hair was pulled up away from her face and she wore her usual jumpsuit. She glanced at him and nodded. Memories of the look of concern in her eyes and a flicker of something else, like maybe interest, as she'd watched him in the hospital drifted through his mind.

Ross had known she was Kody's sister before she'd joined the house. Over the past year they had shared shifts a few times. With him working twenty-four hours on and forty-eight off and her not being able to work the same days as her brother, they hadn't often been on the same schedule. Still, he'd heard talk. More than one firefighter had sung her praises. A few had even expressed interest in her. They had all reported back that they had been shot down. She wasn't interested. There was some speculation as to why, but Ross knew, through Kody, that she was a divorcée. Maybe she was still getting over her broken marriage.

Swinging up on the truck, Ross winced. He had hit something, a door facing or a piece of furniture, on his way out of the burning house. At the hospital they had been concerned with the smoke inhalation and he'd not said anything about his ribs hurting because he hadn't wanted to be admitted. The pain was better than it had been.

He checked a few gauges and climbed out again. This time he tried not to flinch.

Sal came up beside him and said in a low voice, "I saw your face a minute ago. Are you all right? Are you still having trouble breathing?"

"No, I'm fine. I'm good."

She gave him a skeptical look as her eyebrows drew together. "Are you sure?"

"Yeah." If he wasn't careful, she'd make him see a doctor. Did she have that God complex firefighters joked about? The one that went: What's the difference between a paramedic and God? God doesn't think he's a paramedic.

She scrutinized him for a moment. It reminded him of when his mother gave him that look when she knew he wasn't being truthful. "You were in pain a second ago."

He'd been caught. She wasn't going to let it go. Had she been watching him that closely? He'd have to give that more thought later. "I have a couple of ribs that were bruised when I came out of the house."

"Did you tell them at the hospital?"

Now he felt like he had when his mother had caught him. Ross gave her a sheepish look. "No."

"That figures." She shook her head. "You firefighters. All of you think you're superheroes."

He grinned. "Who dares to say we're not?"

She just glared at him. "Feeling like one of those a minute ago?"

He relaxed his shoulders. "I've been wrapping it. I just have trouble getting it tight enough without help."

"You shouldn't be doing that. You need to stop that and just take it easy. Ribs take a while to heal."

"It's hard to do that when you have chores to do at home."

"Don't you have a wife or girlfriend who could help with those?"

"I don't have either." He'd never had a wife. Had come close once but it hadn't worked out.

"Come in here—" Sal indicated the medical area "—and let me have a look. Get rid of that bandage." She didn't wait for him, instead she walked toward the door as if she fully expected him to follow her orders.

Ross hesitated a moment, then trailed after her. He looked back over his shoulder. He didn't need any surprise visits from the bosses just when he was being looked over for more injuries. He hated showing any signs of weakness.

He rarely came to this side of the building. Sal was in the spacious room with a couple of tables and chairs, and a wall of supply cabinets.

She pushed a stool on wheels toward him. "Take your shirt off, then have a seat."

He couldn't do that! She would see his scars. He didn't completely take his shirt off around people for any reason. How to get around doing so had become a perfected art for him. The other morning at the hospital it had been a fight, but he'd convinced first the EMT and then the hospital staff it wasn't necessary to take his shirt off.

She left him to go to a cabinet across the room. Ross took a moment to appreciate the swing of her hips before he pushed his T-shirt up under his arms.

When she returned, she had a pair of scissors in her hand.

"Hey, I don't think you'll need those."

She smirked. "They're to cut the bandage if I need to." She then gave him an odd look but said nothing about his shirt still being on.

He explained, "It hurts too much to lift my arms."

She nodded, seeming to accept his explanation. "Your bandage is around your waist, not your ribs. It wasn't doing you any good anyway."

He gave her a contrite look. "I told you I'd done a poor job of it."

"You're right about that. It doesn't matter. I'm taking it off. And you're leaving it off."

"Is that an example of the tender care I've heard so much about?" Ross watched her closely.

Her gaze met his. "I save that for people who shouldn't know better."

One of his palms went to the center of his chest. "That was a shot to my ego."

She huffed. "That might be so but I'm stating truth. Can you raise your arms out to your sides?"

He winced but he managed to do as she requested. Sal stepped closer. She smelled of something floral. Was it her shampoo or lotion? Whatever it was, he wanted to lean in and take a deeper breath. Her hands worked on the bandage, removing it; her fingers journeyed across his oversensitive stomach. He looked down. Her dark hair veiled her face. It looked so silky. Would it feel that way if he touched it?

No! What was going on? He'd never acted this way around any of the other women he worked with. He hardly knew Sal. She was the sister of one of his best friends. Was he overreacting because he'd not had a date in so long? Whatever it was, it had to stop. His sister wanted to set him up on a blind date. Maybe he should agree.

Sal gathered the bandage in her hand, stepped away from him and dropped the wad into a garbage can.

Ross couldn't help but be relieved, but he was disappointed at the same time. He lowered his arms.

"Okay, arms up again. Show me where you hurt."

With his index finger, he pointed to the middle of his left side. Sal bent closer. Seconds later, her fingers ran over his skin. "Does it hurt here?"

"Yeah."

"I can see some yellowing of the skin. You should've said something at the hospital." She straightened.

Why did she sound so put out? "You've already said that. Besides, the chest X-ray was clear."

She stepped closer. "I'm going to check you out all the way around."

In another place and time, that would have sounded suggestive. And from another person. He and Sal had never had that kind of interaction.

She ducked under his arm and stepped around to his back and then returned to his front before moving away.

Ross missed her heat immediately. He didn't even know her, and he was having this reaction. Why her? Why now?

"If that isn't better in a few days, you need to have another X-ray. You also need to take some over-the-counter pain reliever for the next few days."

Even in a jumpsuit more suited for a male, Sal looked all female. He must have messed up his mind as well as his side in that fire. These thoughts had to stop here.

Her quipping "You can pull your shirt down now" brought him back to reality.

Ross walked toward the door, tucking his shirt in as he went. "Thanks, Sal."

"By the way, I think what you did at that house was both brave and stupid."

CHAPTER TWO

ROSS DIDN'T OFTEN get involved in the social side of the fire department but he was making an exception this time for two reasons. One, the annual picnic was a good place to take Olivia and Jared, his niece and nephew, while they were visiting. Two, it would be nice if he was seen by the bosses interacting positively with his fellow firefighters and the first responders at his station. He needed any edge he could get to gain the promotion.

The event was being held at one of the large parks in town. Not being a family man, Ross had only been to a few of them. There would be the usual fare of barbecue, baked beans, boiled corn and Texas-sized slices of bread. Desserts of every kind and drinks would also be provided. Along with the food were child-friendly games and crafts. Jared and Olivia were excited about the games. He was more interested in the menu; it was some of his favorite food groups.

Ross looked around the area for a parking space. The weather was clear. It would be a perfect day for the event. He scanned the vehicles to see if any belonged to the members of his station. Kody had said he would be there. Would Sal be with him? Why would he care about that? She'd been on his mind too much lately.

Ross enjoyed having the kids around. They came for a weekend now and then, but this time they were staying for a little more than a week while his sister and her husband were out of town. Normally, they would have stayed with his parents but they were off on a cruise. He had sort of volunteered and then been asked to take them for ten days. On the days he worked, a friend's wife had agreed to watch them.

He pulled his truck into a spot in the already half-full parking lot teeming with people. Seconds later, Jared and Olivia were climbing out, their eyes bright with excitement.

"Yay, there's face painting. I want to go over there." Olivia pointed to a tent not far away.

"I want to go ride the pony," Jared said over his sister.

Ross raised his voice above it all. "Circle

up here. We need to have a couple of ground rules. Number one, we stay together, and number two, we stay together. If I lose you kids, your mother and father will be mad at me." He grinned at them. "Got it?"

"Got it!" they chimed in.

"Okay. Why don't we go have lunch first, then we can make the rounds and do anything you like afterward?"

He raised a hand for a high five. Jared and Olivia enthusiastically slapped his palm.

They made their way to the buffet-style line that had formed under a large shelter and joined it.

The kids each held their plates as he served pulled pork onto their sandwich buns. While he was filling his plate with ribs, he looked across the table to see Sal taking some as well. How long had she been there? "Hey, I didn't see you over there."

This was the first time he'd ever seen her in anything but a jumpsuit. Today she was wearing a simple sky blue T-shirt that was tucked into tight, well-worn jeans. A thin belt drew his attention to her hips. She looked fit but not skinny. Her hair flowed down around her shoulders. This version of Sal was very appealing.

Her eyelids flickered and she said shyly, "Hi, Ross. I think you're a little busy to notice much."

"You're right about that." He looked for the kids and found there was a gap between him and them. He saw Sal's grin and forgot what he was doing. He hurriedly returned to picking out his ribs and moved forward. The kids each added a small bag of chips to their plates. When they were all finished, they picked out canned drinks from large containers filled with ice.

When Ross turned around after getting his, he noticed Sal pulling her drink out of a bucket next to his. It didn't appear anyone was with her. Their eyes met and she gave him a soft unsure smile. She looked away over the sea of picnic tables and walked away. Would she have joined them if he'd asked? Did he want her to?

"Come on, kids, let's see about finding a place to sit." He nodded forward. "Jared, head out through the picnic tables that way."

The boy did as Ross said and he and Olivia followed. As they moved along, a number of people he knew spoke to him. He called "hi" and kept moving. Finally, he saw Jared doing a fast walk toward an empty table. Relieved they had found one, Ross settled in for his meal.

He spied Sal weaving through the tables, obviously searching for a place to sit.

She came close enough that he raised his hand and called, "Hey, Sal, come join us. We have room."

Her face brightened at her name, but when she turned his way she looked hesitant, as if trying to figure out a way to refuse, but she came their way.

As she set her lunch down next to Olivia's and across from him, she said, "Thanks. Kody and Lucy are coming but they're running late." She looked around her. "There sure are a lot of people here. I had no idea that it'd be like this." She slipped her legs under the table.

"Austin's isn't a tiny fire department. The families really turn out for the picnic." What was happening to him? He didn't invite single women he worked with to join him for a meal. It was against departmental policy for firefighters and medical personnel at the same station to see each other. But this wasn't a date. He was just being nice.

He wasn't dating right now anyway. In college, he'd dated as much as any of his friends. During the early years of joining the department he'd done the bar scene with some of the other bachelors for a few years but that had got old fast. It was hard to see about the ranch and work his odd hours and keep that lifestyle.

Once he'd been serious about someone, but it hadn't worked out. She'd hated his schedule and had been afraid he might be hurt or killed. After a messy breakup, he'd decided to concentrate on his career and not worry about the aggravation of maintaining a relationship for a while. For now, he'd like to keep things casual, uncomplicated. Maybe after making Battalion Chief he would give serious thought to settling down. But that wouldn't or couldn't include seeing someone he worked with.

"I see." She glanced at Jared and Olivia. "I didn't know you had children."

Olivia giggled.

"This is my niece and nephew. They're spending a couple of weeks with me while my sister and her husband are out of town. Sal, this is Jared and Olivia."

Olivia gave her a curious look. "Your name is Sal? That's a boy's name."

"That's what your uncle calls me at work. My name is really Sally."

His niece wrinkled her nose. "I like Sally better."

Ross did too. It suited her. To think he had never really wondered what her full name was.

Sally looked down at Olivia and smiled. "You know, I do too."

That was interesting. Why didn't she ever correct anybody at the station?

Sally turned her attention to her food and the rest of them did as well. She handed over a napkin to Jared. Ross looked at him. He had barbecue sauce running down his chin.

The boy took it from her.

"Good sandwich?" Sally asked, smiling.

"Yes." Jared grinned.

"I can tell. Mine's good too."

"Uncle Ross's must be good too because it's all over his face." Olivia pointed to him.

They all laughed.

"He looks like a clown," Olivia blurted out.

They all broke into laughter again.

"What?" He wiped his mouth and looked at the napkin. There was a lot of sauce on it.

"It's still on there," Jared stated.

Ross tried again to clean his face.

"It's *still* on there," Olivia said with a giggle.

"You guys are starting to hurt my feelings." Ross liked the sound of Sally's laughter—sweet and full-bodied.

"Here, let me see if I can help you." Sally held up her napkin. "Lean toward me."

Ross did as she suggested as she shifted toward him. Their eyes met and held for a moment. There was a flicker of something there. Awareness, curiosity, interest?

Sally blinked and her focus moved on. A moment later she rubbed a spot on his cheek and sat back.

"She got it," Olivia announced.

However, she had left a warmth behind for him to think about.

"Jared," Sally said a little too brightly, as if she had been affected as well. "How old are you?"

"Nine."

"What do you like? Football? Baseball…?"

Her attention remained on him as if she was truly interested.

"Soccer."

"Soccer. I've watched a few games but I don't know much about the rules."

Ross grinned as Jared lapsed into a full monologue about soccer playing. It hadn't taken long for Sal, uh, Sally to find the kid's sweet spot.

When he ran out of steam Sally was quick to ask, "Olivia, do you have something special you like to do?"

"I like to draw."

"Do you draw people, or animals or landscapes?" Sally took a bite of her sandwich while waiting for an answer.

Olivia wrinkled her forehead. "Landscapes? What's that?"

"Pictures of trees and grass," Jared offered.

"That's right." Sally gave him a smile of praise.

"No, I like to draw horses. I drew a picture of Uncle Ross's horses."

Sally's attention turned to him. She seemed surprised. "You have horses?"

"I do. I own a few acres out west of town."

"You need to come see Uncle Ross's horses

sometime. They're beautiful." Olivia let the last word trail out. "Their names are Romeo and Juliet."

Sally smiled at her. "Are they, now?" She looked at him with a teasing grin on her lips. "Interesting names for horses."

"Hey, they were already named when I bought them."

She grinned. "So you say."

They returned to eating their meals.

As they finished, Olivia asked, "Uncle Ross, can I go have my face painted now?"

Jared turned to him. "And I want to ride the pony."

"We can't do both at the same time. Who's going first?"

Both their hands went up.

Sally covered her smile with a hand.

Ross looked at her and shook his head sadly. "I can handle a company of men at a fire with no problem but give me two kids."

Her look met his. "I think you're doing great."

She did? For some reason he rather liked that idea.

Sally pushed her plate to the center of the table. "Maybe I can help. I can take Olivia to have her face painted while you take Jared to ride the pony. We can meet somewhere afterward."

Ross looked at the children. "That sounds like a plan, doesn't it, kids?"

They both nodded.

He looked around. "Okay, we'll meet over there by the flagpole."

Sally stood. "Then we'll see you in a little while. Olivia, bring your trash and we'll put it in the garbage on the way."

To his surprise Olivia made no argument about cleaning up. Instead she did as Sally asked. As they headed toward the face-painting booth, Olivia slipped her hand into Sally's. She swung it between them.

Sally strolled with Olivia across the grassy area toward the activities. Ross's niece and nephew were nice kids. They seemed to adore him and he them. Her ex-husband, Wade, had never really cared for children. He'd always said he wanted his own but he'd never liked others', thought they were always dirty. More than once he'd worried they would get his clothes nasty when they were around. Thinking back, she didn't understand what she'd seen in him. How she'd even thought herself in love.

Wade had been the local wonder boy. Everyone had loved him, thought he was great. She had too, which was why she'd given up almost everything she loved to make him happy. They hadn't been married long when she'd learned he was having an affair. She'd tried to work it out but Wade wasn't going to change his ways. How had she been so oblivious? What she had thought was real and special had all been a lie. Finally, she'd filed for divorce.

Her judgment where men were concerned was off. All her trust was gone. Never would she be taken in like that again. She mentally shook her head. She wasn't going to ruin a nice day thinking about her ex-husband.

Half an hour later, she and Olivia were on their way to the flagpole. Olivia had a large fuchsia star on one cheek and smaller ones trailing away from it up across her forehead, along with a smile on her lips. Sally couldn't help but smile as well at how proud the girl was.

As they approached the pole, Ross and Jared walked up. The grin on Ross's face when he saw Olivia made Sally's grow. He had such a nice smile. Wide, carefree and inviting. She'd really been missing out on something special by never having seen it before. Most of their interactions had been working ones where there had been no time for smiles.

Ross went down on one knee in front of Olivia. "I love your stars."

Sally watched the similar-colored heads so close together. Ross would make a good father someday. "How was your pony ride, Jared?"

"It was fun, but not as much fun as riding Uncle Ross's horses."

"Can we go play in the jumping games?" Olivia pointed toward the inflatable games set up across the field.

"Yeah, Uncle Ross, can we?" Jared joined in.

Sally looked back at the crowd in line for food. Were Kody and Lucy here yet? She didn't want Ross to think he had to entertain her as well.

"Sure we can." Ross started that way with Jared and Olivia on either side of him. He glanced over his shoulder. "Sally, you coming?"

"Sure." She hurried after them. If he didn't

mind, it would be nicer than just standing around waiting on Kody and his daughter to show up.

As Jared and Olivia played in the inflatable game with the net sides, she and Ross stood outside watching them dive and roll through the small multicolored balls.

After a few minutes of uncertain silence, she said, "Jared and Olivia are really sweet."

"Yeah, I think they're pretty great. Their mom and dad are raising them right."

"Is your sister older or younger than you?" She was more curious than she should be about Ross.

"I'm older, but sometimes she treats me like I'm the younger one. She worries about me being a fireman, or not being married. I know she cares but it does get old."

"I know the feeling. Kody likes to worry over me. My father encourages it as well. I don't know what I'd do without Kody though. He's the one who encouraged me to move out here. Best thing I've ever done."

Kody had told her that she needed to get away from the memories. More than once he had talked about how much he and Lucy liked living here. He'd even tried to get their parents to move out west as well.

"That's right, y'all aren't from around here. You moved out here from North Carolina, isn't that right?"

"Yeah, after my divorce Kody told me there was plenty of work for a paramedic out here. So I decided to come."

"Kody said something about you having been in a bad marriage. I'm sorry."

Sally was too. She didn't take marriage lightly.

"Hey, Aunt Sally."

She turned to see Lucy running toward her with Kody not far behind. Lucy reached her and wrapped her arms around her for a hug. Sally loved her niece. On Sally's days off she often helped Kody with Lucy. Occasionally he needed Lucy to stay over at Sally's while he worked his shift. Sally didn't mind. She enjoyed spending time with her niece. "Hey there. I was starting to wonder where you were."

Kody joined them. "Sorry, the birthday party Lucy was at went longer than I expected." He reached out a hand and spoke to Ross. "Hey, man."

Ross gave Kody's hand a hardy shake. "Glad you made it. Have you tried the ribs yet? They're great."

"Yeah, we just ate, then saw y'all down here. Thanks for taking care of my sister."

Heat went through Sally. She didn't need taking care of. She gave her brother a quelling look. "Kody!"

He acted as if she hadn't said anything as Ross said, "We saw each other and I invited her to eat with us. No big deal." Ross made it sound as if he was trying to explain keeping her out too late to her father.

"Daddy, can I jump?" Lucy pulled on Kody's hand.

"Sure, honey."

Lucy kicked off her shoes and entered the box. Soon she was busy having fun with Jared and Olivia and the other children.

A few minutes later the man monitoring the game told the children inside that it was time to give others a chance. The kids climbed out, put their shoes on and joined them.

Sally put her hand on Lucy's shoulder. "Lucy, I'd like for you to meet Jared and Olivia. Jared and Olivia, this is Lucy. She's my niece."

"Like Uncle Ross is our uncle," Olivia chirped.

Sally smiled at her. "That's right."

A man announcing over a microphone the relay games were about to begin interrupted their conversation.

"Can we go watch, Uncle Ross?" Jared asked.

"Sure. You guys going?" He looked from her to Kody.

"Why not?" Kody responded for them both.

They walked toward the field that had been set up as a relay course. A crowd was already lining up along each side of the area marked with lanes.

"The first race is the egg carry. Children only. Get your spoon and egg and line up."

All three of the kids wanted to participate.

Jared and Olivia were in lanes next to each other. Ross stood behind them. Lucy, with Kody doing the same, was in the lane next to them. Sally stood on the sidelines to cheer them on. The children put the handle of a plastic spoon in their mouth and sat the boiled egg in the other end.

The man said, "You have to go down and around the barrel with the egg in the spoon.

First one back wins. Go on three. One, two, three."

The children took off. Olivia only made it a short distance before her egg fell out. She hurried to pick it up and place it in the spoon again. Lucy and Jared were already at the barrel. Not getting far, Olivia lost hers again. She looked at Ross, her face twisted as if she was about to sob.

With what looked like no hesitation, Ross hurried to her. He went down on one knee and said something to Olivia. He offered her the spoon. She looked unsure but placed it in her mouth. Ross added the egg, then wrapped his arms around Olivia's waist and lifted her. He walked with a slow steady pace toward the barrel. Sally's heart expanded. Ross Lawson was a good uncle. They were way behind the others but the crowd cheered as Ross and Olivia rounded the barrel and headed for the finish line.

They were the last to cross the line but the people acted as if she was the first. Ross placed Olivia's feet on the ground and went down on a knee. The little girl dropped her spoon and egg, and turned around, beaming at Ross. She wrapped her arms around his neck and gave him a hug. What could have been a horrible memory for his niece, Ross had turned into one of joy.

Ross and Olivia joined their little group once more and they watched more of the races, cheering on people they knew.

A little while later the man with the microphone said, "Okay, it's time for the three-legged race. We're going to do something a little different this year to start out with. We need a male and female to represent each fire station. We're going to have a little friendly house-to-house competition. Pick your partner, and come to the line."

"Uncle Ross, you and Sally need to go," Jared said.

"Yeah, you need to," the girls agreed.

"I don't think so." Sally looked around for an excuse not to participate. She received no help from Kody, who just grinned at her.

"Someone does need to represent our station." Ross studied her.

"Go, Aunt Sally." Lucy gave her a little push.

She returned Ross's assessing look. Surely he wouldn't want to do it.

He said with far more enthusiasm than she felt, "Come on. Let's win this thing."

It figured Ross was competitive.

They hurried to a lane. Ross quickly tied the strip of cloth lying on the ground around their ankles. The entire time she tried not to touch him any more than necessary. She wasn't very successful. They met all the way up the length of their legs. Her nerves went into a frenzy when Ross's arm came around her waist. He felt so solid and secure. What was going on with her?

"Put your arm around me," Ross commanded.

With heart thumping harder than normal, Sally did as he requested. Her fingers clutched his shirt.

"Not my shirt, *me*." His words were teasing almost, but demanding, drawing her gaze to his face, which was fierce with concentration and determination. She bit back a laugh as her fingers gripped the well-founded muscle of his side.

"You really do want to win?" she murmured.

He glanced at her with disbelief. "Don't you? We start with our outside leg. You ready?"

"Uh, yeah?" She wanted to run for her car.

The man asked, "Runners ready?"

"Okay, here we go." Ross's voice was intense.

"Go!" the man said.

Ross called, "Outside, inside..."

They were on their way. He was matching the length of his stride to hers. Ross continued to keep the cadence as they hurried up the lane. She tried to concentrate on what they were doing but the physical contact kept slipping in to ruin it. When she tripped, his grip on her waist tightened.

"Outside, inside..." He helped her to get back in sync.

As they made the turn around the barrel, he lifted her against his body as if she weighed nothing. After they had swung around, he let her down and said, "Inside."

Her fingertips dug into his side. Ross grunted, but didn't slow down. His ribs must still be tender. She eased her grip and concentrated on their rhythm again.

The crowd yelled and Ross held her tighter, plastering her against him. They picked up speed.

Between breaths Ross said, "Come on, we're almost there."

Sally put all the effort she had into walking fast. They were near the line when Ross lifted her again and swung her forward with him. The crowd roared as they crossed the finish line. They stumbled hard and went down. Ross landed over her. They were a tangle of arms and legs and laughter.

Ross's breath was hot against her cheek. Her hands were fanned out across his chest. His arms were under her as if he had tried to protect her from the fall. As he looked at her, his eyes held a flicker of masculine awareness. Her stomach fluttered with a feminine response.

"Stay still. I'll untie us." His breath brushed over her lips.

"Well, folks, that was a close one," the man said.

"Aunt Sally, you won! You won!" Lucy's voice came from above her.

"We did?" she grunted as she and Ross worked to untangle themselves from each other.

Ross finally released their legs and stood. He had that beautiful smile on his face again as he offered her a hand. She put hers in his. He pulled her up into his arms and swung her around. "We sure did!"

"Oh." Her arms wrapped around his neck as she hung on. Just as quickly, he let her go. It took her a moment to regain her balance.

Lucy hugged her and Kody slapped Ross on the back. Jared and Olivia circled them, jumping up and down.

"You were great." Ross grinned at her with satisfaction.

She brushed herself off. "Thanks. You did most of the work."

"Okay, everyone," the man said. "There's ice cream for everyone before we have the stations' tug-of-war events."

"I don't know about you guys but I think Sal and I earned some ice cream," Ross said to their group.

"It's Sally, Uncle Ross," Olivia corrected him.

Ross looked at her. "Sally and I, then."

"I've always called her Sweet Pea," Kody quipped.

Sally groaned.

Ross glanced at her and beamed mischievously.

Sally started walking. The three kids joined her. She might never live this day down.

* * *

Ross spooned another bite of ice cream into his mouth. He, Kody and Sally were sitting at a table finishing their food while they watched the kids playing on the park playground equipment. The kids had become fast friends.

He looked at Sally. Her concentration remained on her bowl. She'd really been a trouper during their race. Yet by her expression he'd gathered she hadn't wanted anything to do with it. Was her silent objection to the race or running it with him?

His reaction to having her bound to him had been unexpected. That response had grown and hung like a cloud over them when they had been tangled in each other's arms. There had been a smoldering moment when she had looked at him with, what? Surprise? Interest? Desire? He was male enough to recognize her interest but smart enough to know that she was off-limits, for a number of reasons.

Sally was the sister of a friend. She worked with him. From what he understood she wasn't yet over her divorce and had no interest in dating. More to the point, she didn't strike him as someone who would settle for a fling. As for himself, he couldn't afford to have his mind or emotions anywhere but on his job right now. A real relationship would be a distraction, and something about Sally made him believe that she would be the definition of distraction.

Then there were his scars. More than once they had turned a woman off. A number of women he'd dated had expected a big, strong firefighter would be flawless, would look like a subject of a calendar. They had been disappointed by him.

Thankfully Kody asking him a question directed his mind to a safer topic. A few minutes later the announcer called the tug-of-war teams to the field.

Ross said to Kody, "Well, it's time for the fun to begin. We need to win this thing. I've heard about all I want to about how strong the Twos are." He raised his voice. "Come on, Jared and Olivia, it's time for the contest."

The kids stopped playing and started toward them.

Sally chuckled. "You're really looking forward to this, aren't you?"

"Oh, yeah. All I've heard from Station Two is how they won last year. I'm ready for payback. Do you mind watching Jared and Olivia while I'm pulling?"

"Not at all."

"Lucy too?" Kody added.

"Sure. I've got them all. You guys go on. I'll bring the kids."

He and Kody loped across the field to join the other members of the station. When they reached the part of the field where the tug-of-war would take place, Ross raised his hand. "House Twelve. Here."

Other station captains were doing the same. There was a great deal of commotion as everyone located their fellow companies.

The announcer came on again. "Firefighters and first responders may I have your attention?"

The crowd quieted.

"This is how the competition is going to work. We've set up brackets by pulling station numbers out of a hat. Those will pull against each other. The winner will continue on to the next bracket until we have a winner. Now each house needs to huddle up and decide which six people from your station will be pulling. There must be at least one woman on the team. If your house doesn't have enough people present, then you may recruit from your family members. If you have any questions you need to see Chief Curtis up here. As always, he's our final word."

Using his "at a fire" voice, Ross spoke to the people around him. "Okay, Erickson, Smith, Hart, Kody and me. Rogers, you'll be our designated woman. Does that work for everyone?"

"Ten-four, Captain!" they cheered.

"Great. Now, get into position and get ready to give it all you've got."

Those who weren't chosen went to join those lining the tug-of-war area. Ross and his team moved to the large-diameter rope lying on the ground. A piece of cloth was tied in the middle of it. A chalk line had been drawn across the pulling area.

He glanced over to see Sally and the kids standing near the line. There was excitement on their faces. They all hollered, "Go, Twelves!"

Each team member picked up a section of the rope. Ross anchored at the back where a knot was tied.

The announcer said, "We have our first two teams. The Twelves and the Thirty-Fives. On the word *go* I want you to start pulling. You must keep pulling until the last man is over the line. Is everyone ready?"

"Ten-four!" both teams shouted.

Ross called, "Dig in, firefighters. Let's win this thing." He grabbed the rope tighter.

When the announcer yelled, "Go!" Ross pulled as hard as he could. The grunts of the others ahead of him joined his as they slowly walked backward. The shouts of the crowd encouraging them grew louder. Suddenly there was slack in the rope and he staggered to keep himself upright. They had won. The crowd cheered as his team turned to each other, giving each other high fives.

He would be in pain before the day was done with that much exertion. His ribs had objected when Sally had gripped his side during the three-legged race. With the pulling, they had spoken up loudly again. Still, he was going to do his part to win the tug-of-war. His team needed him. The key was not to let on he was hurting.

Sally and the kids joined him and Kody, giving them their excited congratulations.

Sal said, "Hey, kids, how about helping me get some bottled water for our team?"

"Okay!" all three of the kids agreed.

Sally and the kids hurried away and soon returned with arms filled with bottles. Those standing around took one. Ross finished his in two large gulps. With the next competition about to begin, they moved to the side to watch as the next two teams took the field.

Soon it was time to compete again. They won the next three pulls and were now in the final facing Station Two.

Ross lined up again with his team.

"Go, Uncle Ross, go!" Olivia yelled.

"Go, Twelves! You can do this!" Sally called.

Ross's heart pounded in anticipation as the announcer said, "Go!" On that word he dug his heels into the ground and pulled with all of his might. His hands, arms and shoulders strained. The muscles in his legs trembled with the effort to move backward. Sweat ran into his eyes and still he pulled. His side burned. Clenching his teeth, he tried not to think about it. Concentrate was what he had to do.

The crowd shouted, voices mixing into a roar of encouragement.

Despite the pain he continued to tug. His legs quivered from the effort. Once, twice, three times the team was pulled forward. Only with strength of will did they remain steady and reverse the movement.

He dug deep within himself and called, "Let's take these guys."

With a burst of energy, Ross pulled harder. The others must have done so as well. They made steady steps backward.

Not soon enough for him the announcer said, "And the winner is Station Twelve."

A cheer went up. Ross put his hands on his knees and gulped deep breaths. The other members of the station surrounded them. A bottle of water appeared before his face. He looked up. Sally held it. She gave him a happy smile that made his already racing heart thump harder. All his efforts were worth it for that alone.

"You were great." Her voice was full of excitement.

Ross returned her smile. "Thanks. It wasn't just me. We did it as a team."

"Yeah, but you got them to give their all."

His ego expanded. He had to admit he liked her praise.

Others coming to congratulate him on the victory separated him and Sally.

As everything settled down, the announcer said, "Well, that's all for this year's picnic, folks. We look forward to seeing you next year. Be safe on your drive home."

Everyone slowly drifted off. Their party started toward the parking lot.

"Can I ride piggyback, Uncle Ross?" Olivia asked.

He didn't think his body could tolerate it, but didn't want to disappoint her.

Before he could say anything, Sally suggested, "How about holding my hand?" Lucy already had one of them. "I think your uncle Ross is tired after all that pulling." She gave him a knowing smile.

"Okay." Olivia took it.

Thank you, he mouthed to her.

She nodded.

"We're down this way." Kody nodded, indicating the other end of the parking lot. He gave Sally a quick hug. "See you soon."

Lucy did the same. "Bye, Aunt Sally."

"I better head to my car too." Looking unsure, Sally let go of Olivia's hand. "It was nice to meet you, Olivia and Jared. I enjoyed the day." She started off.

"Hey, wait up, we're going that way too," Ross called.

Sally paused. Olivia took her hand again.

"We'll walk you to your car." Why he'd decided that was a good idea, he didn't know. Sally was fully capable of getting to her car by herself.

"Uh, okay."

He grinned. "You thought you'd get rid of us easier than that, didn't you?"

"I'm not looking to get rid of you." She glanced at him. Her cheeks were pink. "You know what I mean."

He chuckled, then immediately winced.

Her face turned concerned. "Are your ribs still bothering you?"

"You're not going to get all up in my face if I tell you yes, are you?"

Her lips drew into a thin line. "I might."

"Yeah, today's activity didn't help much." He didn't like people seeing weakness in him and for some reason it really mattered that she didn't.

"Have you been taking it easy, until today, that is?" She studied him.

He couldn't meet her gaze. "Well, I've been trying. How's that for an answer?"

She quirked her mouth to one side in disappointment. "When you get home, run a hot bath and soak. It'll help. You do know someone else could have taken your place in the tug-of-war?" There was a bite to her words. She wasn't happy with him.

He grinned. "Yeah, but what fun would that have been?"

She shook her head. "Men. Here's my car. Bye, Olivia and Jared. See you later, Ross."

He and the kids called goodbye and continued on.

Why did he miss her already?

As he was about to start the truck, there was a knock on his window. He jumped. It was Sally. She motioned for him to roll down the glass.

"Hold out your hand."

He did. She deposited some capsules.

"These'll help with the pain. Bye, Ross." She said the last softly.

Something sweet lingered as she walked away. Something better left alone.

CHAPTER THREE

TWO DAYS LATER Ross was in his chair in the office doing paperwork when the ambulance backed into the bay. He watched out the window as Sally came around to the rear of the ambulance. She looked tired. They had already made twice as many runs as the fire side had during the shift.

His company had spent the last few hours washing the trucks, checking the supplies and making sure the station was in pristine order. Now some of the men were in the exercise room working out while others were watching a movie in the TV room.

One of his men stopped at the open door and looked in. "Hey, Ross, it's your turn to cook tonight. Do we need to make a run to the grocery store or do you have what you need?"

Each shift shared kitchen duty. Some stations had one person who liked to do the cooking, while others had a revolving schedule and the crew took turns. His station shared the duty. They assigned two people per shift to handle the meal. His turn had come up. He wasn't a great cook but he could produce simple meals. Mostly he hoped to have someone more skilled than him as his partner.

"I'll check. Who's on with me?"

"Sal."

He'd planned to stay out of her circle as much as possible, spooked as he was by his over-the-top reaction to their time together at the picnic. Cooking a meal with Sally wouldn't accomplish that, but how could he get out of it without causing a lot of questions or hurting her feelings? No solution occurred to him, so he resigned himself to spending time with her. Surely he was capable of that.

During the last few weeks it seemed as if they had seen more of each other than they had in months. In spite of their one day on and two off schedules, he was aware she often worked extra hours in order to have extended time off. What did she do during that time? Why that suddenly mattered to him, he had no idea. He huffed. It wasn't his business anyway.

Ross again glanced into the bay, then back to

the man. "They're just rolling in. I'll give her time to clean up, then go see what she thinks. They've already made a couple of runs this afternoon. I don't know for how much I can depend on her."

"Ten-four."

A few minutes later Ross crossed the bay to the door of the medical area. Sally was going through a drawer. "Hey."

She turned. "Hey."

"Tough shift?"

"You could say that. Two big calls back-to-back." She shrugged. "But you know how that goes."

She was right, he'd had those days as well. "I hate to add to it but we have KP duty tonight. I'd say I'd handle it, but I'm not a great cook."

Sally grinned. "You're not one of those stereotypical firemen who has his own cookbook?"

Ross chuckled. "No, Trent who works over at Tens does. I bought his cookbook to be supportive but that doesn't mean I know how to use it. I could see if one of the other guys wants to help."

"What gives you the idea I'm not any good either?"

He wasn't used to people putting him on the spot and gave her a speculative look. "Are you?"

Her eyes twinkled. "Yeah, I'm a good cook."

Ross wiped the back of his hand across his forehead. "Woo, that's a relief. If we need something, my crew can make a run to the grocery store."

"I have a couple more things to do here, so I'll meet you in the kitchen in a few minutes and we'll see what we've got available. Surely you can open some cans if I'm called out."

"That I can do." He left and headed toward the kitchen.

This was the first time they'd been partnered in any real way. They had each done their jobs during runs but had never really interacted until the picnic. He rather liked Sally. She challenged him even at creating a meal. He wouldn't have thought he would appreciate that kind of confrontation but he did.

He was already in the kitchen area when she showed up. "Any ideas?"

"Let's see what's in the pantry." She opened

the oversize door off to the side and propped it open with a crate, despite the fact the closet was large enough to hold both of them with ease. Was she fearful of being in a closed space with a man, with him in particular, or was there something else? It was just as well he wouldn't ever take a chance on being caught in a suggestive situation with a female at the station. Having that on his record would ruin any chance for advancement. This promotion was important to him, his opportunity to make a real difference.

It had been while he was in the hospital after the fire that he'd decided one day he would help people as that firefighter had helped his grandpa. As soon as Ross had graduated from high school, he'd joined the same volunteer fire department that had saved them. He'd continued to do so while he was in college. After that, he'd joined the Austin Fire Department. He loved everything about being a fireman.

In some odd way, he was determined to outdo fire. To be smarter than it. Learn to anticipate its next move. He wanted to control, conquer it so no one else would ever have to live through those moments of fear he'd had.

Sally ran her fingers down the canned goods stacked on a shelf. "Yeah, I think we have enough here for vegetable soup. Corn, beans, chopped potatoes and tomato juice. Two tins of each should do it and we can always make grilled cheese sandwiches."

He pursed his lips and nodded. "That sounds good."

Ross stepped to the doorway but didn't enter. Their meal would have to feed six firefighters and two medical support techs.

"Is there any ground beef left over, or roast beef in the freezer or the refrigerator?" she asked as if she'd been thinking along the same chain of thought.

"I'll check." As he walked across the kitchen, he could hear the clinking of cans being shifted.

After rummaging through the freezer for a moment, he announced, "Yeah, there's two or three pounds of ground beef."

"Pull it out to thaw. It can go into the soup," she called from the closet before she appeared with her arms full of cans. She dumped them on the counter as he placed the beef in the sink.

"There's a couple more cans in there. Do you mind getting them?"

He went to the closet and retrieved the cans sitting off by themselves. "Are these them?"

"Yeah."

With his foot, Ross pushed the crate back into the pantry and let the door automatically close before going to the counter. He put the cans beside the others. "What now?"

Sal looked at him with her hand on a hip. "This is a partnership, not a chef/sous chef situation."

"I prefer the chef/sous chef plan." Ross grinned.

"You act as if you don't do this often."

He leaned his hip against the counter. "I don't, if I can get out of it."

"Okay, since you've designated me to be the chef, I'm going to put you to work. Start by opening all the cans. You're qualified on a can opener, aren't you?"

"I can handle that. It's electric, isn't it?"

Sally laughed. "Yeah. It is." She turned her back to him. "And they let him be captain of a company."

Ross pulled the opener out from under the counter. "I heard that."

Pulling a large boiler out from under the cabinet near the stove, she put it on a large unit and turned it on. Ross opened cans and set them aside as he covertly watched Sal uncover the still-frozen meat and place it in the pot. She worked with the same efficacy that she used in her medical care.

"So you just have that recipe in your head? Carry it around all the time?"

Sally glanced over her shoulder. "I made it for my family all the time growing up." She tapped her forehead. "I keep it locked away right here."

"Well, I have to admit I'm impressed. I had no idea you had such skills."

"I'm not surprised. We really haven't worked together much."

Ross sort of hoped that would change even as he sternly told himself, yet again, he wanted no interferences in his life right now. Socializing with a female he worked with would definitely qualify as that.

"It's nothing but meat and a few cans of vegetables." She turned serious. "But the secret ingredient is Worcestershire sauce. Would you mind checking the refrigerator door and see if there's any there?"

He did as she requested. "There's half a bottle."

"That'll be enough." Her attention remained on what she was doing. "We'll make it work. Is there any ketchup, by chance?"

Ross opened the refrigerator door again. "Yeah, there's some of that."

"Then bring that too."

"Ketchup?" He'd never heard of such a thing.

"It'll add a little thickness to it and also a little sweetness."

"You really are a chef."

"It takes more than ketchup soup to make you a chef."

A loud buzz followed by a long alarm then three shorts indicating it was their station being called ended their conversation. Ross was already moving as Sally turned off the stove and put the pot into the refrigerator along with the open cans.

As they ran down the hall toward the bay, the dispatcher's voice came over the loudspeakers. "Two-car accident at the intersection of Taft and Houston. One car on fire."

Moments later Ross was sliding his feet into his boots next to his crewmates. He jerked up his pants and flipped the suspenders over his shoulders. It took seconds for him to pull on his turnout gear that had sat ready on the bay floor. Grabbing his coat, he swung up and into the passenger seat of the engine, while the other firefighters got into their seats behind him. He secured his helmet with the strap under his chin.

One of his men was assigned the job of pushing the buttons to open the huge overhead door. The driver hopped in and they wheeled out of the station with the siren blaring. His company worked like a well-oiled machine. They were out the door in less than a minute. They had four to get to the scene. This economy of effort was another of his leadership qualities that hopefully would get him an edge on that promotion.

Sally and her crewman were right behind them. The traffic pulled to the side and stopped, allowing them to go by. At the lights they slowed then continued on. The goal was not to create another accident in their speedy effort to get to the first emergency.

As they traveled, Ross was on the radio with dispatch, getting as much information about the accident as possible. His heart rate always rose as the adrenaline pumped and thoughts of what to expect ahead raced.

They pulled up to the accident but not too close. Sally and her partner did the same. Ross's stomach roiled. The driver's-side door of one car was smashed. It had been the center of impact. The passenger door behind it was a mangled mess but standing open. A child-size jacket hung halfway out the door and a doll lay on the road.

Smoke bellowed from the hood of the other car and oil covered the area. His job was to get the fire contained and put out. Thankfully there was no gas spreading.

"We need a fire extinguisher up here. Spread for the oil."

As his men worked with the fire, he could see that at least the car seat remained intact inside the first car and the child was gone. Looking about, he could see Sally's partner assessing the kid, who looked about four years old. The bigger issue now would be getting the woman who was still wedged in the front out.

Another ambulance arrived.

Ross continued to give orders and his men

moved to follow them without questions. They knew their duties and went to work. He moved closer to the car to see Sally climbing into the back seat.

"What do you need?" he asked.

She didn't look at him. "We're going to need the Jaws of Life to get her out. The car is crushed so badly the front doors won't open. I suspect the driver has internal injuries. We need to get her out right away."

Using the radio, Ross said, "Rob, we need the Jaws of Life. Jim, you help him."

The men rushed to the supply truck. Ross looked at Sally again to see her securing a neck brace on the woman. All the time she was re-assuring her patient she would be fine, and her child too. He walked away long enough to see that everything was under control with the other car. The driver was sitting on the curb, dazed but otherwise looking uninjured. One of the EMTs from the second ambulance was seeing to him.

A couple of his firefighters were rerouting traffic along with the police.

He rejoined Sal as his men with the heavy-duty machine returned to the car. They inserted the mouth of the instrument into the area where the doors met and the machine slowly pushed the two apart. It took precious minutes. The metal creaked as it bent and groaned as it shifted. Finally, the firefighters were able to separate the doors.

"We need the gurney over here," Sally called, then said over her shoulder to Ross, "We'll need some help getting her on it."

Ross and another firefighter moved into position, while she and another EMT stood across from them.

"I want us to slowly move her out, scooting her along the gurney." This was Sally's area of expertise and he would follow her lead.

Minutes later the patient was in the box with Sally in attendance and sirens blaring, headed toward the hospital. Ross and his company went to work seeing that the vehicles were loaded on wreckers and debris was cleared from the road.

By the time Sally finally made it back to the station kitchen, she found Ross stirring the soup, which bubbled gently on the stove. He was more talented than she had given him credit for.

"Hey, I'm glad you could join me. I thought I was going to have to take all the glory." He grinned at her. The kind that caused a flutter in her middle. Why him? Why now? He was a nice guy. The kind she might be able to trust. She shook her head. If it was another time in her life, she might be tempted.

She smirked. "Like I was going to let that happen."

"You were right. Looks like I can brown meat and dump cans of vegetables." He sounded pleased with himself.

"Turns out you have more talent than you let on."

"Some say that about other areas as well." His comment sounded offhand but she suspected there might be more to it. Was Ross flirting with her? No, that wasn't possible. What if it was? She had to stop thinking like that. There was nothing but trouble down that road.

Suddenly self-conscious, she cleared her throat. "So where were we before we were so rudely interrupted?" She pulled the loaf of bread that was sitting on the counter toward her. "I'll get the grilled cheeses ready. Everyone must be hungry." She started buttering bread.

"What're you doing there?"

"Making fast and easy grilled cheese sandwiches. Pull out one of those large sheet pans, please." Sally kept moving the knife over the bread as she spoke. "Then get the sliced cheese and start putting it on the bread. We'll slip it into the oven, put it on broil, and we should have grilled cheeses in no time."

Ross went to work without question. Soon they had the sandwiches browning. "I'll get the plates, bowls and things while you go tell everyone soup's on."

"Are you always so bossy?" Ross asked as he exited the kitchen.

Did he really think she was dictatorial? She never thought of herself as being that way. Yet Wade had complained she was always on his case. Toward the end of their marriage, she guessed she had been. Wade hadn't ever been at home. More often than not he'd been between jobs; either it wasn't the right one or he was too smart to work with the people around him, or some other excuse. His parents had raised him to believe he could do no wrong.

She'd dreamed of being a doctor all through high school but after she and Wade had married he'd not wanted his wife going to school. He'd said school took up too much of her time. Time she could be spending with him. He'd never been a fan of her working as a paramedic, but she'd refused to give up volunteering when she'd been needed so badly by their rural community. That was the only thing she had defied him on. She had wanted their marriage to work.

Looking back, she could see how selfish Wade really was. That had certainly been brought home when she'd learned he was having an affair. But where she'd really messed up was not seeing through Wade before she'd married him. Her judgment had been off, so caught up in the fantasy rather than the reality. Next time, she'd be more careful about who she opened her heart to.

Ross returned with the other firefighters on his heels. Over the next hour the company shared a meal, told stories and laughed. When the meal was over, she and Ross cleaned up, each thankful that most of the dishes went into the dishwasher.

Ross was washing the last of the pots when his phone rang. He shook off his wet hands and pulled the phone out of his pocket. He moved away from the sink and Sally stepped into his spot. She was tired and still had paperwork to take care of. Hopefully they wouldn't be called out anytime soon.

As she rinsed off the pan, Ross said with a disappointed note in his voice, "I'll work something out." He paused. "No, you can't help it," he said, before saying his goodbyes and hanging up the phone.

Sally hesitated to say anything, afraid it might be wrong, but didn't want to appear unsympathetic. "Everything all right?"

"No, not really. The lady I have watching Olivia and Jared while I work? Her mother has had an accident and Marcy has to go help her. That leaves me having to find someone to help me out."

"Would swapping shifts help?"

He was scrolling through the numbers on his phone. "Naw, I've got a meeting with the Chief. One I can't afford to miss." Ross spoke more to himself than to her.

"What day are you talking about?" Sally dried her hands on a dishrag.

"This Friday." He still wasn't giving her his attention.

"I'm not on the rest of the week. I have too much overtime. I'll watch them. If you don't mind Lucy joining us."

"Hey, if you'd do that it would be great. Jared and Olivia would love to have someone to play with."

"There's only one problem." She paused until she had his attention. "I don't think three kids are going to be happy overnight at my place. It's too small. I guess I could ask Kody if we could go there."

"Y'all can come to my place. There's plenty of room there. A lot of space outside to play. Plus, Jared's and Olivia's stuff is already there."

"Are you sure?"

He took the pot from her and put it under the cabinet. "Of course I am. You're doing me a favor."

Sally wasn't sure that going to Ross's house was a good idea. It seemed as if they were getting too friendly. Yet her place was so small and Kody's would be a little tight for three active kids as well. She didn't see another good choice. "That would probably be best."

He studied her a moment. "I'll owe you big-time for this."

"Don't worry about it. It sounds fun. The kids and I'll have a good time together."

"If you could come out around eleven, that should give me time to show you around then get to town in time to start my shift. I'll text you my address." He headed out the door.

"Hey, don't you need my number?"

He looked bashful. Cute, in fact. "I guess that would be helpful."

"You don't arrange childcare often, do you?"

"Nope." Ross grinned. "It's a fine art I'm just now learning."

She gave him her number. He punched it into his phone, then he was gone.

CHAPTER FOUR

SALLY HAD MADE a serious mistake by agree-
ing to watch Ross's niece and nephew. Doing
so was another step into further involvement
in Ross's life. Being together at the picnic had
revealed she was far too attracted to him. An
attraction she neither wanted nor needed. She
must stay focused. Still, she liked the guy.
The last time she'd been this enamored with a
man, she'd been devastated. That mustn't happen again. She wouldn't allow it. The upside
to the day's arrangement was that Ross would
be at work the entire time.

And she would be with the kids...

In his home. His personal space. She hadn't
thought that through either. She would be
where he lived. Touching, sitting and sleeping
among his personal belongs. No, she hadn't
considered that part of this agreement at all.
She should have done so before she'd blurted
out her willingness to help. Yet helping out a

fellow firefighter went with being a member of that family. It was just what a team player did in an emergency situation.

Ross had texted her his address as promised. Sally had picked up Lucy from Kody's house on her way to Ross's. Lucy had been so excited about seeing Jared and Olivia again she couldn't get in the car fast enough. The idea of an overnight stay had heightened her anticipation. She'd chatted most of the way about all the fun they would have. Sally certainly hoped so. The closer she came to Ross's house, the tighter Sally's nerves knotted. She hadn't acted this way over seeing a man in a long time. Control—she needed to get some over her wild emotions.

The drive was ten miles out of town to where the land rolled gently, the trees were tall and the fields green. When she had moved to this part of the country, it hadn't taken long for her to fall in love with Texas. Even though she liked her apartment, she wished she could find a place with more outdoor space.

The day was beautiful with the sun shining in a blue sky as she turned the car off the two-lane highway onto a dirt lane. On either side were fenced pastures with a few trees here and there. The lane ended at a white clapboard house with a porch along the front. Large oaks shaded one side and the lawn surrounding the house was neatly mown. Behind it there was a small red barn with a couple of horses in the corral.

She sighed. When she got her medical degree, this was just the type of place she would look for. There was something restful, comforting about it. A place someone could find contentment. She loved everything about it, immediately.

When she'd taken Kody up on his suggestion to move to Texas, she'd realized how right he'd been. She'd had no trouble getting a job and there had been something cathartic, cleansing, about leaving all the ugliness of her marriage behind and starting over again. It had taken some time, but she'd finally settled in, had decided on a plan and was now focused on seeing it through.

Soon after arriving in Austin, she'd enrolled in college and finished her degree. Sally smiled. To think she was studying to take her MCAT now. If she did well enough, she hoped to enter medical school in the fall, while continuing to work part-time at the firehouse when she could. She wasn't going to let anyone or anything divert her this time.

As she climbed from the car, Ross stepped out of the beveled glass front door.

A warmth washed over her. Especially not a man with striking blue eyes and a hunky chest.

He came to stand beside a wooden post of the porch. He wore his usual fire station uniform of navy pants and T-shirt with the department logo on one breast. Practical work boots completed his attire. He appeared healthy and fit. His welcoming smile made him even more handsome than she remembered. Her stomach quivered. She had to get beyond this fascination with Ross. Still, couldn't a girl enjoy a moment of admiration for a man?

He drawled, "I see you found us."

Returning his smile, she gathered her purse. She'd bring in her MCAT study books after he'd left. Lucy had already hopped out of the car and gone to meet Jared and Olivia, who were in the side yard.

Ross came down the wide steps. His agile movements reminded her of a panther she'd once seen in a zoo. "Are you ready for this?"

"What if I said I wasn't?" She glanced at him as she gathered Lucy's and her overnight bags.

He grimaced. "I don't know what I'd do."

She grinned, looking at the kids. "I'm going to be fine. We'll all be fine."

"Here, let me get those for you." He reached for the bags.

"Thanks." His hands brushed hers and she quickly pulled away. The physical contact had intensified her growing nervous tension.

They walked side by side to the house. Happy laughter from the kids filled the air. Ross moved ahead of her and hurried up the steps. Tucking Lucy's bag under his arm as he reached the door, he opened it and held it. She strode by him, making sure they didn't touch. If they had, would he have felt the same electric reaction she had when their hands had met?

The room Sally entered was dim and it took a moment for her eyes to adjust. Only a few feet inside the door, she looked around the large open space. The high ceiling was supported by dark beams. The walls were a cream color complemented by a gleaming warm wooden floor. It was furnished with a brown leather sofa and two armchairs along with an old chest she assumed he used as a coffee table. A TV hung over the mantel of a stone fireplace.

In the back of the house was the kitchen. A large bar separated it from the living area. A table for four sat to one side. Windows filled the corner, giving a beautiful view of the barn, trees and the fields beyond. Everything was neat, but masculine.

This was a man's abode. Ross's. Sally shivered. She had truly entered the lion's den.

Ross set the bags down beside a door to a small hallway and walked farther into the house. "Come on in. Let me show you around. As you can see, this is the kitchen." He pointed toward the hallway. "Over there are two bedrooms. Jared and Olivia are in them. Olivia has the one with the twin beds so there's an extra bed for Lucy. On the other side of the house is my room. The sheets on the bed are clean. Ready for you."

Her breath caught. Her eyes widened. Finally she blinked. "I, uh, think I'll just sleep on the sofa. That way I'll be closer to the kids in case one calls out." Spending the night in Ross's bed would be far too...personal? Uncomfortable?

Nerve shaking? Lonely? Whatever the word was, she wouldn't be doing it.

"I want you to be comfortable. I think you'd be happier in a bed. It's the only one I have that's available." He shrugged. "But all that's up to you." She made no comment and he continued, "You can find all kinds of movies and games in the cabinet beside the fireplace. The kids know where everything is."

She nodded.

"I've already ordered pizza for dinner tonight. It should be delivered at six. Right, here's the tip." He tapped some bills on top of the counter. "My number is on this pad if you have any questions, anytime."

Sally moved closer to look.

"There should be plenty of sandwich fixings in the refrigerator. I also have peanut butter and jelly. Chips. And drinks."

Her smile widened as she softly laughed.

His look turned serious. "What's so funny?"

"You are."

"How's that?" He watched her too close for comfort as if he didn't want to miss any change in her expression.

"Firehouse Captain turned Mr. Mom."

He chuckled. One that started low and rough then slowly rolled up his throat and bubbled out. "I do sound a bit that way, don't I?"

"You do, but it's nice to know there're supplies, I'll give you that. Thanks for taking the time and thought to make it as easy as possible for me."

"You're welcome." He picked keys up off the counter. "I'd better get going."

She followed him out onto the porch.

"Oh, I forgot. Could you see that the horses are fed tonight and in the morning? Jared knows what to do." He moved to the porch railing and called, "Jared and Olivia."

Both children stopped playing and looked at him. "I don't want you giving Sally any trouble. If she needs help, you do so. No argument about bedtime either."

"Yes, sir," they called in harmony.

He smiled and nodded. "Good. I'll see you tomorrow."

"Bye, Uncle Ross." Olivia waved.

"Yeah, bye," Jared said as an afterthought as he ran for a ball.

Ross turned to her. "I really appreciate this."

"You've already said that."

"I know, but I do." He walked to her, stopping just out of reach. His gaze met hers. A spot of heat flushed through her middle that had everything to do with his attention. "Well, I'll see you tomorrow around one." He went down the steps.

"Okay."

He hadn't made it to his truck before he said, "Call if you have any questions."

"I will." Sally wrapped her arm around the post he had stood beside earlier and leaned her cheek against it. She watched him leave. Ross put his hand out the window and waved. She stayed there until he was out of sight.

What would it be like to have someone who wasn't eager to leave her? That she could say bye to who would look forward to returning to her. At one time she'd believed she had that. Instead Wade had acted as if coming home to her was a chore. Why had he married her if he hadn't really wanted her? In less than a year he had been off with someone else.

She wanted a man who desired her. That she was enough for. Maybe one day she would try again, but that wasn't going to happen anytime soon. She had plans, dreams. That was what she should be thinking about. She was better off without the obstacle of a man in her life for the time being.

Yet here she was seeing to Ross's niece and nephew. At his house. When he'd driven away, it had seemed as if they were husband and wife and she were seeing him off to work. But that wasn't reality. She was the babysitter and nothing more. And she didn't want anything but that.

Lucy interrupted her troubling thoughts with, "Aunt Sally, we're hungry."

"Well, it's about lunchtime. Come on in."

The kids stomped up to the porch.

"Let's go see what we can find in the kitchen."

After lunch they returned to playing. The pizza Ross had promised arrived just as he'd said it would and they ate it picnic style under one of the oak trees.

The sun was low as they finished then went to feed the horses. Jared took the lead. First, he turned on the hose to add water to the trough. Sally grinned at his puff of importance as he went into the barn to get grain. He returned with a gallon tin can full and let each of the girls dump a part of the feed into two buckets for each of the horses.

As Lucy took her turn, she hit the rail with the end of the can. It went flying and landed in the water trough. She gasped and tears filled her eyes.

Sally placed a hand on her back. "It's okay, hon. We'll get it."

"I'll do it." Jared started pulling his shirt off.

Sally looked at him in dismay. "What're you doing?"

"It'll get wet if I don't take it off." He handed her his shirt, then leaned into the trough far enough that his head almost touched the water. When he straightened pulling the can out, the water inside spilled all down his front.

Sally laughed. "Obviously you knew what was going to happen."

Jared grinned, dropped the can on the ground and took his shirt from her. "Yeah, we drop it in almost every time we visit."

"How come a boy can take his shirt off and a girl can't?" Lucy asked.

This wasn't a discussion Sally wanted to get into, especially with other people's children. She just had to keep the answers simple. "Well, because boys and girls are different. Especially when they get older."

"Uncle Ross is a boy and he never takes his shirt off," Olivia announced. "Not even when he's swimming."

What was she to say to that? "Guys don't have to take their shirts off if they don't want to."

"When it's hot I like to take mine off." Jared picked the can up and headed for the barn.

Olivia's statement left Sally curious. She'd have thought a man with Ross's physique should be proud to show it off.

Lucy took Sally's hand. "Sometimes when I'm playing with the water hose, I take mine off."

It was time to change the subject. "Let's go get a bath and have a snack before bedtime."

By just after dark, Sally had all the kids in bed. She wasn't sure who was happier, them or her. She'd had less active days at work. Plopping on the couch, she stretched out her legs, letting her head rest on the pillowed leather behind her. Sally closed her eyes and sighed. She and the kids had had a nice day. They were a good tired and she was as well. While she was trying to convince herself to get up and do some studying, her phone rang.

Digging in the back pocket of her jeans, she fished it out.

"Hey, how's it going?" Ross's rich voice filled her ear.

Her heart did a little pitty-pat. "We're doing great. Have you been worried about us?"

"More about you. Two kids can be a handful so I can imagine three's more difficult."

He had been thinking about her? "Everybody's fine. They're all in bed now." She yawned.

"I bet you're thinking about going as well." The timbre of his tone suggested ideas better left locked away. She sat straighter. "I'll be up for a little while longer."

"I really thank you for this."

It was nice to feel useful to a man to whom she was attracted. For so long she'd felt unworthy. In the end duped and rejected. "You don't have to keep saying that. How did your meeting with the Chief go?"

"Really well."

He'd asked her some personal questions, so

she felt entitled. "Do you mind if I ask what's going on?"

"No. It's just that I'm on the shortlist for Battalion Chief. I've been trying to make a good impression. Not being there when the Chief's making his rounds wouldn't have been good."

"You'll make a great Battalion Chief." Of that she had no doubt.

"I don't have the job yet."

"Maybe not yet, but you'll get it." He was good at his job and others noticed. She certainly had.

"The competition is pretty strong. I've worked with all of them at one time or another."

"I can't imagine anyone being more qualified than you." And she couldn't.

"Thanks, Sal, for that vote of confidence. It means a lot." Ross's voice held a note of gratitude.

She couldn't stem her curiosity about him. "Have you always wanted to be a firefighter?"

There was a pause. "Yeah, ever since I was a little boy."

"That's a long time." Her amazement rang in her voice. They shared something in common.

They both had known what they wanted to do since they were young.

"I'm not that old." He chuckled.

"You know what I mean. What made you want to be a firefighter?"

This time he didn't falter before answering her. "I saw firefighters at work when I was a kid and I decided then that I want to help people like they did."

She almost said *aww* out loud. "That's very admirable. Was it a bad fire?"

"The worst. My grandfather's house was a total loss." His voice had grown rougher with each word.

She could tell that it had been a life-changing event for him in more than one way. "Oh, Ross. I'm sorry. I hope he was all right."

"He was. He rebuilt. You're sitting in his house now. He left it to me when he died a few years ago. I've made some updates."

Sally looked around. "I like your house. I want something like it one day."

"I'm happy there." There was a pause, then he said, "Tell me something, are you going to sleep in my bed tonight?"

Heat flowed hot and fast throughout her body.

Her mouth went dry. Ross coming on to her. She liked it.

The buzz of the fire station alarm going off, then the dispatcher speaking, was all she could hear for the next few seconds.

"Gotta go," Ross said. "See you tomorrow." More softly, as if a caress, he finished with, "Take care, Sweet Sally."

"Bye," she said into an empty line. Sweet Sally? She liked the sound of that coming from Ross.

Ross neared the end of the drive to his home with keen anticipation. He was coming home to someone. Was his life really that isolated? Not until this moment did he realize how much he liked the idea of having someone waiting on him at home. He'd looked forward to seeing Sally and the kids. Hearing how their time together had gone.

He grinned. Maybe now he'd get an answer about where she'd spent the night. It still shocked him that he'd dared to ask. Had called her Sweet Sally. After all, she was doing him a favor and he'd hit on her. He hoped things wouldn't be strained between them now. He should have kept that question to himself. In a twisted way he was relieved to have been out on a run most of the night. At least he hadn't had time to think about her in his bed—without him.

He'd put taking a real interest in a woman on the back burner for so long his reaction to Sally was unsettling. Did he dare take a chance on her? Gambling on how a woman would respond to his scars, he'd kept most of them at arm's length. He'd let Alice in but that hadn't ended well either.

Maybe it was time for him to think about more than his job. Still, the idea of living through major rejection again struck him with fear. Was it Sally in particular or just that it was time for him to try again that had him thinking this way?

He parked his truck next to Sally's car, then grabbed his duffel bag.

The kids were playing right where they had been when he'd left the day before. They called hello as he climbed the steps. A fireman's schedule with the staggered hours had always seemed like a difficult schedule for a family to live around but there was something nice about the idea of having children. What had caused that idea to pop into his head? He'd been satisfied with Jared and Olivia's visits and hadn't thought of having his own children in a long time.

These days he was having all sorts of odd thoughts.

As he entered the house, he was tempted to call, "Honey, I'm home," but he didn't think Sally would appreciate his humor. An amazing aroma filled the air. There was food cooking in the oven. Sally's back was to him as she chopped something.

Her hair was pulled up in a messy arrangement, yet it suited her. She wore a flowy top of some kind and jeans. There were sandals on her feet. There was nothing special about her clothes, yet the combination made her appearance fresh, simple and disturbingly sexy.

Music played softly from the radio. She swayed and hummed along. It was strangely erotic. His blood heated. He wanted to walk up behind her and pull her back against him. Leave her in no doubt of his need for her. How would she react to him kissing her neck?

Not a good idea. At all. Tamping down his desire, Ross cleared his throat. "Hey."

She turned and smiled. "Hey. I didn't hear you come in."

He walked toward her, sniffing. "I'm not surprised. What's that wonderful smell?"

"My father's favorite meat pie. I thought since we've had sandwiches, pizza and cereal that we should have a real meal. We voted to wait on you."

He could get used to this. "Are you saying what I left wasn't nutritious enough?"

She shrugged. "I'm not complaining. I like to cook and it's nice to do it for more than just myself."

"You're welcome to cook for me anytime." He met her look and held it.

Her gaze turned unsure as she said, "Will you call the kids in and tell them to wash their hands while I get this on the table."

"Sure thing. Let me put my bag up first." Yes, he liked coming home to Sally, the kids and a meal. He sure did.

Picking up his bag, Ross went to his bedroom. Sally hadn't slept there. Nothing had been moved and he had no doubt that her scent would have lingered. For some reason these days his body picked up on every detail of hers despite his best effort not to notice. The idea she had slept on the sofa bothered him. She should have been comfortable at his house.

Stepping to the bath, he saw that she hadn't been in there either. He didn't know much Shakespeare, but he did think maybe the woman did "protest too much." He grinned. Maybe she was more affected by him than she wanted to admit.

He went outside to call the kids. After a good deal of noise and shuffling around, including adding a chair to the table, he and the kids were seated. Sally placed a bowl of salad on the table and joined them.

He looked at Sally. Her face was rosy from being in a warm kitchen. Tendrils of her hair had come free and fallen across her cheek. She pushed at them with the back of her hand. She was lovely. "It looks wonderful, Sweet Sally."

Olivia giggled. "It's just Sally."

He waved his hand over the table. "Don't you think she's sweet? She did all this for us. I sure do."

The kids chorused their agreement.

Sally giggled and her color heightened. "Thank you."

This was a real family moment. The type of thing he'd not given a thought to having in a long time. He liked it. Found himself wanting it more often.

The kids spent the rest of the meal talking about all they had done while he was gone. Sally remained quiet, listening and smiling. Not once did she make eye contact with him, despite the fact he was sitting across from her. Was she afraid of what she might see or what he might find in her eyes? He'd have to give that more thought.

After their meal was over, she said, "Kids, please carry your plates to the sink, then you may go back out and play. Lucy, we'll need to be leaving soon."

They did as she asked without an argument, which Ross couldn't believe. When they were gone, he turned to her. "How do you do that?"

She stood and picked up her plate. "Do what?"

He gave her an incredulous look and pointed with his thumb over his shoulder. "Get them to do something without back-talking?"

She shrugged and carried the plate to the sink. "I'm a woman of many talents."

"I don't doubt that." Some of those he'd like to explore.

Sally began filling the dishwasher. Ross brought the rest of the dishes off the table to her. They finished straightening the place together.

"We make a pretty good team in the kitchen." Ross returned the dishrag after wiping the table off, trying to keep his mind off the other things they might be good at together.

Sally dried her hands and hung the dishcloth on a knob. "Seems that way."

Ross noticed a stack of books at the end of the bar and walked over to see what they were. He placed a hand on them. "Are these yours?"

"Yes." Sally picked them up and hugged them against her chest as if protecting them. "I don't want to forget them."

"This says MCAT on it. Are you studying to take the test to be a doctor?" He didn't even try to keep his surprise out of his voice.

"Yeah. I'm trying to get into medical school."

He leaned a hip against the counter. "I'm impressed. I had no idea." How had he not heard talk at the house? "Is it a secret?"

Sally shook her head. "No."

Apparently, he'd been so caught up in his wish of being Battalion Chief he'd not noticed that about her. What kind of boss would he be if he didn't see more outside of his own world? He needed to do better. "So, when's the test?"

"Two weeks from today."

"Good luck."

"I'm afraid I'm going to need it."

"I doubt that. I think you'll make an amazing doctor." And he did. The more he knew about Sally, the more captivated he was by her.

Her eyes were bright. "Thanks for that. I hope I do."

He gave her his best encouraging look. "I've no doubt you will."

"Thanks, that's nice to hear. I've always dreamed of being a doctor."

"Is this your first time taking the test?" Ross was far too interested in her life, but he couldn't stop himself from asking.

"Yes."

"Why haven't you done it before now?"

"My husband didn't want me to go to school. He wanted me to be there when he came home."

Something close to anger boiled within Ross. The dirtbag hadn't even supported his wife's dreams. Kody had said he was a jerk, but Ross had had no idea how big of one.

Ross heard the laughter of the kids. "I'm sorry. I'm sure you didn't get much study time here."

"I did some this morning while the kids were playing. When I get home, I'll go at it hard. Only thing is that they're replacing the siding on my apartment complex, so I'll have to work around that. Speaking of going, Lucy and I need to be doing that."

Ross was reluctant to see her leave. He found he really didn't like that idea.

"You're welcome here anytime. I mean, it's quiet here. You can come out anytime, whether or not I'm here."

"I don't know…" She looked uncertain.

He raised a hand. "Hey, just know the offer's there if you need it."

"Thanks. That's kind of you." She gathered her books and left them at the front door before she stepped outside and called, "Lucy. We have to go now."

"Do we have to?" Lucy whined.

"Yes. Your daddy's expecting you, and I have studying to do."

Ross joined her with her bags in hand.

She grinned at him. "So much for my talents."

He laughed. She reached for their belongings. "I'll carry them to the car."

The kids came up on the porch.

Olivia pointed her small finger toward the rustic star nailed over the door on the beam above his and Sally's heads. "Look, Uncle Ross, you and Sally are standing under the Texas star. You have to kiss her!"

Ross had forgotten about the star. It was a game he'd been playing with Olivia since she was a baby. Before she left from a visit, he gave her a kiss under the star.

"When you're standing under the star, you have to kiss the one you're with. Isn't that so, Uncle Ross?" Olivia gave him an expectant face.

Sally's eyes had grown wide. "What?"

Ross spoke to Olivia. "Yeah, but that's between you and me. It's not for everyone."

"But you kiss Mom and Grandma under it," Olivia insisted.

"I, uh, don't think that's necessary." Sally took a step away.

"That's not what you said, Uncle Ross," Jared said. "You said you must always tell the truth."

"I did say that." He was caught in a trap and he was afraid Sally was as well. He looked at her. "You wouldn't want me not to be a man of my word?"

"It seems I have no choice." She didn't sound convinced. In fact, she acted as if she'd like to run. Yet she put the bags down and placed her books on top of them.

He took her hand and led her back to where they had been standing under the star. She must have been in shock because she offered no resistance. He placed his hands on her waist. Their looks met. He said softly, "You do know it won't be a fate worse than death, don't you?"

"I'd like to think so."

He kissed her, stopping any further words with his mouth. Her lips were soft and warm. Everything he had imagined and more.

Sally's hands came to his waist and clutched his shirt as if she needed him as a stabilizer. After the first seconds of indecision, she returned the kiss. His body hummed as his hands tightened with the intention of pulling her closer. This kiss was too sweet, too revealing, too little. It had quickly gone from an intentioned friendly kiss under the star to one of passion.

"Ooh."

"Ick."

"Ugh…"

The sounds coming from the kids made him draw back. Ross looked into Sally's eyes. She appeared as shaken as he. He registered the shiver that ran through her. Sally broke from his hold and he didn't stop her.

"Lucy, we need to go." There was a quiver in Sally's voice as she grabbed her books.

He reached for the bags before she had time to pick them up and followed her to the car. She opened the door and without looking at him said, "You can just throw those in the back seat."

"Will do. Thanks again for helping me out."

"You're welcome. Lucy, buckle up." Seconds later she and Lucy were ready to go.

Ross stood out of the way as Sally turned the car around and headed down the drive. He watched her go with his body still not recovered from their kiss. By the way Sally had acted, she'd been as affected as he had been. One thing was for sure, he wanted to kiss her again. If he had anything to say about it, it would happen again—soon.

CHAPTER FIVE

FEWER THAN THREE days had passed but that wasn't enough time for Sally to erase the memory of Ross's lips against hers. In fact, she'd relived those moments over and over to the point where it had disrupted her study schedule. Yet another example of how letting a man into her life again could derail what she really wanted. She had to put an end to the daydreaming.

Doing well on the MCAT was too important. Instead of focusing on questions and the correct answers, she had been thinking of the tingling sensation having Ross's arms around her had generated and the throbbing in her center as he'd kissed her. She'd been aware of their attraction but had had no idea how electric it was until his lips had touched hers.

Would Ross try to kiss her again? She had to stop thinking about him.

She had to focus on her studies, work around her emotions as well as the construction being done on her apartment complex. With air hammers going off constantly and the banging of siding falling, she'd quickly learned she couldn't get any studying done at home.

She'd tried waiting until the workmen quit for the day but that had left her studying well into the night. Once, she'd gone to a coffee shop but even there she had become too distracted. The library had been her last resort, but the chairs weren't comfortable after an hour or two. She needed her own little nest, a place to spread out her books. What she wanted was for the work on her apartment complex to be completed, but that wasn't going to happen anytime soon.

Now she was dragging her books into the fire station, hoping it would be a slow shift so she could get some studying time in. Pulling her bag out of the car, she headed inside. She groaned long and deep. Ross's truck was in the parking lot. He was working today. She took a deep breath, trying to settle her heartbeat.

Unfortunately, he was the first person she saw. The living, breathing diversion in her life. To make matters worse, she ran straight into him as he circled the back of the engine while she walked between it and the rescue truck. He grabbed her shoulders, but quickly let go and stepped back. Even that brief touch was enough to set her blood racing.

"Are you okay?" His eyes searched her.

"I'm fine," she answered around a yawn.

He studied her closer. "You sure? You look tired."

"Thank you. That's what every woman wants to hear." Her voice was overly haughty.

"Hey, that wasn't a criticism, but concern."

She shifted her bag. "I'm sorry. I'm just a little on edge. And tired. It's not your fault. I shouldn't take it out on you." Though some of it *was* his fault.

His voice turned sympathetic. "What's the problem?"

"I've been trying to study and they're working at my apartment complex. It's so noisy during the day I've been staying up late at night. I've taken all next week off to study but I don't see things getting better. I've got to find someplace quiet to concentrate."

"I told you you're welcome out at my place."

Sally's breath caught. What was he suggesting?

Ross must have seen her look of astonishment because he hurriedly raised a hand. "Hey, it's not what you're thinking. I have to be at the training center all next week. So I'll be working eight to five. The kids are with my parents now. You'd have some peace and quiet to study. By the time I come home in the evenings, they should be done for the day at your place."

It did sound like a doable plan. An exceptional one. "That's really nice of you. But I can't put you out like that."

"You won't be putting me out. I won't even be there. How could you disturb me?"

Ross made it sound as if she would be stupid not to agree. It'd be better than skipping around from one place to the other trying to get some real studying done. Just the thought of sitting on Ross's porch swing as she worked had its appeal. Yet...

She shook her head. Things between them were already too... She couldn't put a word to it. Didn't want to. Going to his house again would only make them more involved. "I don't know. I'm sure I'll figure out something."

"This is what I'm going to do. I'll leave a key under the mat. If you want to go, go—if you don't, don't. Just know you're welcome."

One of the firefighters called out to him. "See you later, Sally."

He didn't give her another look, as if they were two old friends and didn't have that kiss hanging between them. Maybe it hadn't been as big a deal to him as it had been to her.

After doing her usual shift routine, she managed to get in a few hours of study before the intercom buzzed and the station was called out on a run.

She and Ross shared no conversation outside of what was essential during the accident. She left at noon the next day and returned home to find the construction trucks parked in front of her building. She ground her teeth. This just wasn't the time in her life for this. She had to find some quiet. It would be another week of bangs and clangs but now they would be right outside her walls. Her test was only four days away. She'd taken time off work to cram all she could into her brain but how much of that could she get done here?

The idea of sitting on Ross's swing with a breeze blowing and the horses in the pasture popped into her mind. The image was too sweet. She might ace the test if she studied there.

When Ross had suggested she go to his house, she'd had no intentions of doing so, but with the men working on her building in particular it seemed silly not to. If she timed it right, she could arrive just after Ross left for the day and leave before he came home. The worst that could happen was that he'd come home early. Then she'd make an excuse and leave.

The next morning Sally loaded all her books and notes into the car and headed out of town. She needed quiet and Ross's place offered that. If it meant she had to push away her anxiety over using his place to get quality time in her books, then she'd manage it. The bigger picture was more important. Just turning up his drive eased her nerves.

His home looked just as inviting as it had before. She climbed out of the car. More than that, it sounded as serene as she had hoped. The only noises were from chirping birds and the occasional snort of a horse. Filling her arms with books, she climbed the steps to the porch. She placed her armload on a small table near the swing.

Going to the door, she glanced at the star hanging above and refused to give it any more thought. Doing so would waylay her plans for the day. She didn't have time for *what if*s and *maybe*s. All her plans, dreams and hopes were concentrated on what would happen on Saturday. She must be prepared.

Just as Ross had promised, the key was under the mat. Unlocking the door, she filled a large glass with water, returned outside and set the glass on the table. She picked up a book and settled on the swing. Using the big toe of one foot, she gradually started it to moving.

Time passed quickly and it was soon lunchtime. She'd brought her food and enjoyed it on the porch. Needing to do something to give her mind a rest, she decided to cook Ross dinner in appreciation for giving her this great place to study.

She found enough in the pantry to put together a small chicken casserole and a dessert. Leaving a note of thanks for Ross on the counter, she made a list of items to buy on the way home for tomorrow's meal and returned to studying.

The next days passed much as the first one.

By Friday afternoon, Sally felt confident about the test ahead. She'd managed to get a great quantity of quality studying done. She'd be forever grateful to Ross.

His truck came down the drive as she was on her way to the car to leave. Her breath caught and her heart beat a little faster. He was early.

Ross pulled up beside her, his window down. "Hey, I was hoping I'd see you before you left. I wanted to wish you luck."

"Thanks. I could use all I can get. I really appreciate you letting me come out here. I don't know what I'd have done if I hadn't."

He put his arm on the window opening and leaned out. "Hey, I'm the one who should be thanking you. The meals have been a nice treat. I'll miss them."

"You're welcome. It's the least I could do." She opened her car door.

"How about sharing dinner with me tonight?" His words didn't sound as confident as she would have expected them to.

Sally considered it for a moment. She was tempted, but she needed to keep her focus. Get a good night's sleep. Be prepared for tomorrow. Not be distracted. And Ross was undoubtedly a distraction. "Thanks, but I'd better not. I need to get home. Get ready for tomorrow. I have an early morning and even longer day and I still have notes to check." Now she was overselling her decision.

"I understand. Maybe another time." There was a note of disappointment in his voice.

"Maybe." She couldn't afford to give him encouragement. Or herself any either. She moved to get into the car.

"Good luck tomorrow. I know you'll do great."

She gave him a tight-lipped nod as she climbed into her car. "I sure hope so."

He called, "Hey, Sweet Sally, I have faith in you."

She liked that idea. Wade had never encouraged her or made her feel confident. That Ross did bolstered her spirit. She felt special. Something she hadn't experienced where a man was concerned in a long time.

Ross had spent the day doing chores around the place and wondering how Sally was doing on her test. Why it mattered to him so much, he had no idea. Possibly because he knew it mattered to her. He was beginning to care too deeply for Sally. The last time he'd let someone in it had ended badly but for some reason he couldn't seem to resist Sally's pull.

He was glad that he could help her by giving her a place to study. The meals had been a pleasant surprise each evening. It had been fun to guess what would be waiting on him next. He feared he could get too accustomed to having a hot meal waiting on him. He'd probably gained five pounds over the week. Because of Sally his home seemed warmer and more inviting.

More than that, knowing Sally had been thinking about him had gotten to him on a level he didn't want to examine. Damn, he had it bad. He was starting to think like a sappy teenager.

What he should be doing was thinking about being Battalion Chief, planning what he wanted to say at his interview. He would tell the review committee that he wanted to use the position to help implement new and innovative firefighting techniques. He knew personally what fire could do to a person's life and he wanted to make positive changes where he could. For Austin to become a world-renowned department who used cutting-edge practices. As a member of the higher ranks, he could help make that happen. Maybe help keep a boy and his grandfather from ever being hurt in a fire. He hoped to help change the department for the better and, more important, save lives. That was what getting promotions had always been about for him since he'd started working at the fire department.

Finished with all he had planned to do for the day on the ranch, and thinking through his ideas for the interview, Ross still couldn't get Sally out of his mind. That afternoon he cleaned up and drove into town. He went by the farm supply store to pick up a few items. After making a couple more stops, he ended up at the fire station. Kody was working. Maybe he had heard from Sally. Just how long did one of those tests last?

He and Kody leaned against Ross's truck talking about nothing and everything. More than once Ross was tempted to ask him about Sally but stopped himself. He didn't want to be that obvious about how involved he was in her life.

"Lucy had a great time at your house the other day. Sally said she enjoyed it as well. I had no idea you were such a family man." Kody grinned.

He'd enjoyed their time together too but he wasn't going to let Kody know that. "I don't know about that. I'm pretty sure Sally got the short end of the stick. She did all the work. Three kids to watch is a handful."

"From everything she said, she had fun. She couldn't say enough about how much she liked your place." Kody sounded as if he were making casual conversation but for some reason Ross questioned that.

"Yeah, she came out this past week to study while I was at the training center."

Kody gave him a speculative look. "She didn't tell me that."

Ross shrugged. "She said she needed a quiet place to study, and I offered."

Kody's eyes narrowed. "She didn't say anything to me. Didn't ask to use my place."

It was Ross's turn to grin. "You don't expect her to tell you everything. You do know she's a grown woman?"

"Yeah, but I'm her big brother. It's my job to

know what's going on. She's had a hard time of it."

"Little overprotective, are you?" Ross would be as well if Sally belonged to him. That wasn't going to happen. He couldn't let it. Still…

Kody huffed. "She says the same thing." He gave Ross a direct look. "I'm just concerned about her. She's been hurt badly in the past. I'd hate for her to go through that again."

Ross held up a hand. "Hey, you're jumping the gun here. We're just friends."

"I'm just sayin'—" Kody's phone rang and he pulled it out of his pocket, looking at the number. "Speak of the devil." Into the phone he said, "Sweet Pea." There was a pause, then, "Yeah." A pause. "Really? Call the auto club and have it towed in. Can you get a taxi home? I hate it but I'm at work."

"What's going on?" Ross asked. He sounded more concerned than he should have.

Kody studied him a second. "Sally's car won't start."

"I can go." He was already heading to the driver's door.

Kody looked a little surprised. "Okay." He said into the phone, "Ross is coming after you."

There was quiet. "No, he offered. He's right here. He should be there in about twenty minutes. You get in the car and lock it. Don't open it for anyone except the tow driver or Ross."

"Tell her to stay put. I'm on my way. You text me the address." Ross hopped into his truck.

Ross shouldn't have been as happy as he was that Sally was having car trouble but it gave him an excuse to see her.

He made the drive in less than twenty minutes. Sally's car was parked near a walkway into a large glass-and-brick building on the Austin State University campus. There were only a few other cars in the lot. She was waiting in the car just as Kody had told her. When he pulled up, she got out. Wearing a light blue button-down shirt, jeans and ankle boots, Sally looked younger and more vulnerable than he knew she was.

She gave him a weak smile. "I appreciate you coming."

"Not a problem. I was at the house when you called. What seems to be wrong?" Sally looked exhausted, as if she had been through the mental mill.

"I don't know. It just wouldn't start. I've

called the auto club and they're on their way but it'll be another forty minutes or so."

"Do you mind giving it a try?"

"Okay." She turned the key. The engine just made a grinding noise.

Ross opened the hood and moved the battery cables. He leaned around and called, "Try it again."

The car acted as if it wanted to come to life, then nothing.

Ross closed the hood as he shook his head. "You just got all my mechanical knowledge."

This time she grinned. "I guess it's a good thing the tow truck is on the way."

"Come on over to my truck and we'll wait there." He held the passenger door open for her.

Sally acted reluctant for a moment but gathered her purse and joined him in the truck.

Once inside he turned so he could see her face. "So how do you think you did on your test?"

She sighed deeply. "It was harder than I thought it would be. I don't know how I feel about it. I guess all that's left to do is cross my fingers."

He crossed his. "Mine'll be as well."

Sally rested her head back on the seat and closed her eyes. "I'm just glad it's over. I'm exhausted."

"When was the last time you had something to eat or drink?"

She opened her eyes to slits. "We had a lunch break, but I was too nervous to eat much."

"You stay put. I'm going to that convenience store across the road to get you a drink and something to eat. When we've taken care of your car, we'll stop and get you something more substantial." He opened his door and climbed out. "Lock the door while I'm gone. I'll be right back."

Sally murmured something but he suspected she was already half-asleep.

Ross made a quick walk across the parking lot to the store. When he returned, Sally was just as he'd assumed she would be—sound asleep. Her chin hung to her chest and she softly snored. Climbing in as quietly as possible, he gently put an arm around her shoulders and brought her head to his shoulder. She settled against him. Everything about the moment seemed right.

He pushed his disappointment away when all

too soon the tow truck arrived. "Sally, wake up. The tow truck is here."

She moaned and burrowed closer to him, all warm and sweet.

"Sweet Sally, come on, wake up."

"What?" She blinked, looking perplexed.

"The tow truck is here."

She quickly sat up and shifted away. "Oh, yeah. Sorry."

"No problem."

She scooted out her door. He stepped out, joining her and the tow driver.

Half an hour later they were back in his truck and on their way.

Ross glanced at Sally. "I'm going to get you something to eat. Do you have a preference?"

"I want a big juicy burger." Just as she answered, thunder rumbled. The sky had been slowly darkening.

"Consider it done."

Ross pulled into the first fast-food place he came to and into the drive-thru line. While they were waiting for their food, the wind picked up. Thunder rolled and lightning flashed in the sky off to the west.

"Sally, I know you've had a tough day but

would you mind if we run out to my place for just a moment before I take you home? The horses are out and in this weather they get nervous. I hoped it would go north of us but it doesn't look like that's going to happen."

He handed her their bag of food as she answered, "I don't mind. With a nap and a burger, I'm ready to go. If I'm not, I need to learn to be, if I want to be a doctor."

She'd already finished her sandwich by the time they were on the outskirts of town. Ross glanced at her and grinned. "Good?"

There was no repentance in her smile. "I was starving."

He chuckled. "Would you like to have my other one?" Ross held up a second burger, still in its wrapper.

"No, that's not necessary," she said in a sassy tone. "But I'll have some of your fries if you aren't going to eat them."

"Well, that figures." He placed his container on the seat between them.

"What do you mean?" Her complete attention was on him. He liked it that way.

"They're the best thing you can order at that place. I like my fries super crispy."

"I do too." She plopped the last one of hers into her mouth and reached for his.

As they turned onto his drive, large raindrops hit the window shield. Angry lightning split the sky.

"Looks like it's going to be an ugly one," Sally said. "These are the kind of days that go by so fast at the house you don't know if you're coming or going. More traffic accidents than you can count."

Ross laughed and pulled the truck to a stop. "I've had more than my share of those days too. This shouldn't take long. The key is still under the mat. Make yourself at home. I'll be back in just a few minutes."

Sally watched Ross sprint off around the house toward the barn. The rain was coming down harder. Thunder and lightning were filling the sky in a regular rotation as she ran to the porch. She opened the door, going in and turning on a light. Stepping to the large picture window at the back of the house where the table was located, she searched for a glimpse of Ross at the barn.

She continued to look out the window as the

storm grew. The rain fell hard enough to make it difficult to see. Minutes ticked by, enough she started to worry something had happened to Ross. Just as she was about to go out after him, he came through the back door in a burst of wind and water.

Grabbing a dish towel, she hurried to him and handed it over.

"Thanks." Ross took it and wiped his face.

"A tree came down on the fence. The horses are out. I've got to go after them and fix the fence. I'm sorry about this. You're welcome to stay here, or I can call you a taxi?" He pulled a kitchen closet door open. Rubber coats hung inside it. On the floor were mucking boots. Ross grabbed a jacket and boots, then went to a chair and started putting on the high-top rubber shoes.

Sally picked up a pair as well.

"What're you doing?" Ross gave her an incredulous look.

"I'm going with you." She sat at the table and started removing her shoes.

Ross returned to gearing up. "You don't need to do that. You've already had a long day."

"I'll survive. You don't even know where the horses are. You're gonna need help."

Ross opened his mouth.

"I wouldn't even bother arguing. I'm going." She pulled on a boot. It was too large but she would make do.

He grinned. "Figures."

As he shrugged into his coat, she picked out one and did as well.

"Ready?" Ross took two large flashlights off the shelf in the closet.

Sally pulled the cap up over her head. "Ready."

He nodded and opened the door.

She could hardly see with the storm blocking what little of the sun was still up. The angry sky made what light there was a spooky haze of yellow green. At least it wasn't completely dark. She didn't want to go crazy in front of Ross. Her silly childhood fear wouldn't impress him. At least having the flashlight would help her keep her sanity.

The rain blew sideways as she braced herself against the wind. It didn't take long for it to blow her cap back. She would just have to get wet. Ross headed toward the barn. She followed. As they went, she saw one of the giant limbs from the oak in the side yard had fallen on the fence.

"What're we doing in here?" Sally shook her coat as she entered the barn, relieved to get out of the wet for a moment. Her hair was drenched and the front of her jeans soaked.

"I wanted to get a couple of halters and leads." Ross went into a small tack room.

"Where do you think we'll find them?"

He called out to her as he moved around in the room. "I don't know. If the fence was up, I'd say in the trees out in the pasture. With the fence down, I'm not sure. I'm going to try out by the road first. I can't afford for them to cause an accident. In this weather cars can't see them."

Ross's concern was evident in his voice. He soon joined her again, carrying what he had come after. He handed her one of the halters. "This won't be a fun trip."

"I've done un-fun things before. Ready when you are." She wasn't going to let him stop her from helping, especially after he'd done so much for her.

"Hopefully they didn't go far." He had a resigned look on his face as he lowered his head and left the barn.

Sally joined him. He led the way down the drive. The wind let up some but the going was still difficult as they trudged along with their flashlights moving in a back-and-forth pattern in the hopes of seeing the animals. As they came to the paved road, there was still no sign of the horses. She could sense, by the hunch of his shoulders, Ross's frustration and concern. He moved the beam of light wider.

"I'm going to check those trees across the road," he shouted.

"Okay." She joined him and pointed her flashlight that way. There, standing under the trees, were the horses.

They sidestepped as if nervous as she and Ross approached.

Ross put his hand out, indicating she should hang back. He slowly approached them.

Sally could imagine him speaking softly to them. She'd bet he did the same when he made love. Ooh, she needed to concentrate. Thoughts like that did nothing to keep Ross in the friend slot where she had placed him.

Ross waved her forward. He handed her a

lead attached to the halter on Juliet and took the halter she carried. She'd been right. He talked to Romeo the entire time he worked. It was solid and reassuring. Something she missed in her life.

"Ready?"

She nodded.

"Hold the halter and the lead." He demonstrated. "If there's more lightning, they may balk. They're pretty skittish."

Sally made sure to place her hands in the same position that Ross used. She'd been around horses some but never under these conditions. As Ross had suspected, the sky did light up again. Both Romeo and Juliet jumped and flinched but she managed to keep Juliet under control. Romeo reared but Ross soon calmed him.

"Let's get them in the barn." He started toward his place and she kept pace.

They made it to the barn without any more mishaps. Being in the dry again was like heaven. Slinging her wet hair out of her face, she looked at Ross. He was every bit as wet as she and it only made him look sexier.

He grinned. "Well, I'm glad that's over."

Sally couldn't agree more.

Ross led Romeo into a stall. She waited. He soon joined her and took Juliet to another stall.

When he returned this time he said, "I'll still have to go out and see about the fence. Do you mind giving them a couple of cups of oats? You'll find it in the tack room."

"I'll take care of them." Sally pushed at her hair but a strand stuck to her cheek.

Ross, using a finger, moved it away from her eyes. Their gazes met. "You were great out there, Sweet Sally." His hands went to her waist and he pulled her to him. "What would I do without you?"

For a second she thought he might kiss her. Thought how it would warm her from the inside out as a hot drink did on a cold night. This close, Ross smelled of rain, earth and healthy male. Alive.

But instead he let her go and left the barn, leaving a honeyed heat coursing through her veins.

Ross had expected Sally to go to the house when she'd finished with the horses but instead she stayed outside to help him. He had pulled the truck over so he could use the headlights to work by. Thankfully the rain had eased.

As he used the chain saw to cut limbs off the tree branch that had broken the fence, Sally pulled the debris out of the way. Wet and with the high pitch of the chain saw ringing in their ears, they worked side by side. They soon had the worst of it off the fence.

Ross cut off the saw. "Why don't you go on in the house and clean up? I have to get some tools and get this fence back into place. I'll finish the cleanup later. I'll be in soon."

"I can help you." She kept pulling limbs.

Was there anything that Sally couldn't do or wouldn't do? She was a special person. He put the saw in the shed and found the tools he needed to repair the fence. When he returned, she was still cleaning up the area.

Ross started removing the broken barbed wire.

Sally came to him. "What can I do to help?"

He picked up a tool. "Do you know how to handle a claw hammer?"

She lifted her chin. "I sure do."

He'd given up on encouraging her to get out

of the weather. "Then go to the next post and start taking out the staples."

While he worked on replacing the wire on his post, Sally went to the next one. He joined her and she moved on to the next one. She was good help but he wasn't surprised by that, though he was thankful. Because of her he wouldn't be out all night repairing the fence.

An hour later she held the wire as he hammered the last staple into place.

"That'll do it until morning." Ross picked up his tools.

"Give me those. I'll put them away while you move the truck." Sally reached for the toolbox.

Ross let her have it and off she went to the shed. He found her again just inside the kitchen door, struggling to remove her boot. "Hey, let me help you with that. Hold on to the counter and I'll pull it off for you."

"It has been winning." She leaned her butt back against the counter, held on and lifted her foot.

Ross tugged and the boot slipped off. "Okay, the other one."

Sally lifted her other foot. He pulled that boot

off as well and dropped it on top of the first one with a thump.

"You want help with yours?" she asked.

"No, I can get them." He started working his boot off. "What I'd really like is for you to head to the shower."

"I know you're used to giving orders—"

"All I want is for you not to get sick. I'll bring you some warm clothes to put on."

She put her hands on her hips and gave him an indignant look. "I'm made of stronger stuff than that."

He grinned. "I've no doubt of that, but just so I don't have to worry, humor me. Please? You're welcome to my shower or you know where the spare one is."

Sally glared at him for a second, then turned and walked toward the guest bathroom.

Disappointment jolted him. He wished she'd chosen his—with him in it.

Ross shucked off his clothes in his bathroom and pulled on a pair of shorts and a T-shirt. Going to his chest of drawers, he found a T-shirt and sweatpants for Sally.

He knocked on her bathroom door. The sound of running water reminded him that the only thing between him and a naked Sally was the door. He swallowed, then called, "There's some clothes on the floor for you."

"Okay, thanks."

Ross returned to his bathroom, turned on the shower to cold instead of hot.

When he came out to the living room again, he didn't expect to find Sally lying on his couch asleep. He shouldn't have been surprised. She'd had an emotionally hard day taking a life-changing test, then to have car trouble, wrangle horses and fix a fence in a storm. She'd withstood more than most and remained in a positive mood as she'd done them all. She had the right to fall asleep.

He quickly checked the station schedule on his phone to make sure she wasn't on duty the next day, then went to the spare bedroom to turn back the covers. Back in the living room, he lifted Sally into his arms, noting how slight she was for a woman with such a strong will. He carried her to the bed, covered her up and tucked her in. After a moment of hesitation, Ross placed a kiss on her forehead. "Thanks for all your help, Sweet Sally."

Ross had had hopes for a more satisfying kiss tonight. He had to admit he was disappointed. But Sally needed rest. He went to the kitchen looking for a snack. Opening the refrigerator, Ross searched it for some ideas. As usual, there was little there but he did have one more plateful of the last casserole Sally had made for him. He dished it out, warmed it in the microwave and sat down to watch a sports show.

Between shows he started their dirty clothes in the washing machine. He rarely had women's clothes joining his. There was something intimate about his and Sally's clothes comingling. Erotic and right at the same time.

Before going to bed, he went out to check on the horses. They were secure but thunder rolled in the distance. They were in for another round of bad weather. Inside again, he looked in on Sally. She was sleeping comfortably on her side, her hands in a prayerful manner under one cheek. Leaving the door ajar, Ross went to his room. He climbed into bed. Would he be able to sleep knowing Sally was just steps away?

Sometime later the sound of screaming jerked him awake. For a moment Ross was disoriented until he remembered that Sally was across the house. His eyes darted to the alarm clock on his bedside table. It was blank. The electricity was off. A scream ripped the air again. This time he had no doubt it came from Sally.

Rushing across the living room, he worked his memory not to stumble into the furniture. Too late he realized he hadn't paused long enough to pull on shorts or a shirt. He was only wearing his boxers. There was no time to turn back. Sally needed him.

Another shriek caused ripples down his spine. She sounded terrified.

Lightning flashed and he could see her huddled against the headboard. Her head was down in the pillow she clutched to her chest. She was sobbing and shaking in panic like a wounded animal.

He took a few steps into the room. "Sally, it's Ross." He kept his voice low so as not to scare her further. "I'm right here. Everything's okay. You're at my house. The electricity is off."

Lightning lit the sky once more.

Her eyes opened. There was a wild look there. They remained unfocused. She didn't recognize him. He moved to the bed. "It's Ross. It's going to be okay. I'll get some candles."

She gripped his forearm, her fingers digging in. "Don't go! Don't leave me."

The fear in her voice went straight to his heart. This was a side of Sally he'd never seen. He suspected few had. "Sweetie, I'm just going after candles. I'm coming right back."

"No." Her grip tightened. He'd have finger-nail marks in the morning.

Ross sat on the bed and pulled her into his arms. Rocking softly, he said soothing nothings to her just as he had to the horses earlier. Sally seemed to ease. "I won't leave you."

Why was Sally so scared of the dark? She'd always acted so invincible.

He couldn't leave her, but they couldn't stay here all night. The bed was too small for both of them. If either one of them was going to get some rest, they had to go to his bed.

"Sally, I'm going to get up now. I'm going to carry you to my room. Hold on."

She made an unintelligible sound as he stood and lifted her into his arms. As she clung to him, he picked his way to his room without any missteps. He placed her on the side of the bed he'd been on and tucked the covers around her. Even in the darkness of the room he could see that her eyes were shifting from side to side with distress. "I'm going after candles. Just into the bath. I'll be right back."

In a weak voice she whined, "You won't leave me?"

"Sweetie, I'd never leave you. I'll be right back."

He hurried to the bathroom to gather the fat candle and matches he kept there for power outages. Placing the candle on the bedside table, he lit it. That little bit of light in the dark room removed most of the fear from Sally's eyes.

"Hold me." The words were low and sad.

She didn't have to ask him twice. He slid under the covers beside her and pulled her close. She shifted into him, sighed and her breath soon became warm and even against his neck.

CHAPTER SIX

SALLY WOKE TO the sun shining through the window of a room she didn't recognize. Her back was against a solid wall of heat. She moved her hand. Her palm brushed across coarse hair on the muscled arm around her waist.

A shiver of panic ran through her. Slowly glimpses of waking in the dark, terror absorbing her, Ross coming to her, then him carrying her to his bed settled in her mind.

Oh, heavens, she'd begged him to hold her.

Could she have embarrassed and humiliated herself more? She was a grown woman afraid of the dark. At her house she was prepared for events like the one last night. She always had a flashlight next to her bed and one in the kitchen and living room. In an unfamiliar place, she had come undone. How was she ever going to face him?

The mattress shifted beneath her. It was

going to happen sooner rather than later. She moved to slip out from under Ross's arm.

"Sally, are you awake?" His voice was rusty from sleep, making him sound terribly sexy. Worse, he sounded worried about her.

How was she going to explain her bizarre behavior?

She continued to slide across the sheet until she was out of touching distance and as far away from him as the bed would allow. She was grateful it was king-size. She put her feet on the floor and turned from the waist to face him. At least she was still wearing the T-shirt and sweatpants he had loaned her. That gave her some armor in this uncomfortable state of affairs.

Ross quickly pulled on a T-shirt. The bedsheet covered his lower half. He was decent, yet she was too aware that moments earlier she had been in his arms, against his bare chest. He lay on his side with his head propped on his hand, waiting and watching her.

"Mornin'," he drawled, as if it were a regular occurrence to have her in his bed.

"Good morning." Sally paused. She must be the one to address the elephant in the room. Adjusting her position for comfort while searching his face, she reluctantly added, "Thanks for helping me last night. I guess you're wondering what happened."

"I'd like to hear the why, but right now I'd like to know if you're okay." He watched her too closely. As if he was gauging her emotional stability.

"Yes, yes, I'm fine, except for being extremely embarrassed." She glanced out the window to the side of the house. From here she could see the damaged part of the fence and the barn. The sky was clear. It all looked so peaceful now. A complete one-eighty from the upheaval in her.

"I'm sorry I had to bring you to my bed. I hope you haven't taken it the wrong way. We both wouldn't fit in that smaller bed and you wouldn't let me go. We needed someplace to sleep."

Heat washed through her. The best she could tell, the section of his bed they had been sleeping on was approximately the same size as the bed in the other room. Had she moved next to him? Or had he stayed close to her? It didn't matter now. What did matter was that it should not happen again. Even if it had been nice to wake up to.

"It's okay." She tried to make it sound far more insignificant than it was to her. "You don't owe me an explanation. I know I was acting crazy."

He lifted a corner of his mouth. "I'd go with 'out of character.'"

Sally winced. "You're being kind. I think *crazy* is accurate."

"I'd like to know what happened, but only if you want to tell me." Curiosity was written all over his face as he waited, his eyes not leaving her.

She crossed her legs and settled more comfortably on her side of the bed. Ross had a way of putting her at ease even when she didn't like the subject.

"When I was a kid, a group of us were playing hide-and-seek. I hid in a trunk. One of the kids thought it would be funny to lock me in. I was stuck there for hours before my mother found me. Now I'm terrified of the dark and small spaces. Silly, I know. My ex-husband used to make fun of me all the time."

A dark look covered his features. "I don't

think it's silly. Everyone's scared of something. They may not show it, but it's there anyway."

"Yeah, right. Like you're afraid of anything. I've seen you run into a burning building."

His look was unwavering. "I assure you, I am."

"Like what?" It was suddenly important that she know. Ross seemed invincible to her.

He shifted, acted unsure, not meeting her eyes. It was as if he had said more than he'd intended. But sharing her own fear had made her realize how important it was for him too. "So tell me. What're you afraid of?"

"You aren't going to let this go, are you?" His words were flat.

"No. You know my secret. I promise not to share yours."

"Turn your head."

It was an order but she did as he requested. The mattress lifted, letting her know Ross had stood. What was he doing?

"You can look now." Ross was wearing a pair of shorts and walking toward the window on his side of the room. He spoke to the window-pane. "I don't make a habit of telling this. In fact, I don't ever tell this."

Sally moved around the bed to sit where he had lain. It was still warm.

"Remember I told you about the fire that took my granddaddy's house?"

"I do." She'd thought of that boy many times.

"There was more to the story."

She held her breath. This wouldn't be good.

"As I was coming out of the door of the house, part of the ceiling fell on me. My shoulder was burned."

Sally sucked in her breath.

"I have some ugly scars as reminders of that night." His shoulders tensed.

She wanted to reach out to him. "So that's why you always wear a shirt. I'm sorry, Ross, I had no idea."

"Few people do. Like I said, I don't share this with everyone." There was an emotion in his voice she couldn't put a name to. Disappointment? Fear? Uncertainty?

"Why're you telling me?"

"Because you wanted to know, and I didn't want you to think you were the only one with hang-ups."

Goodness, he was a nice guy. Sally had forgotten that there were men who had compassion for others. She arose and went to him, placing a hand on his shoulder. "Thank you for trusting me with your secret."

He flinched.

Sally took a step back. She shouldn't have touched him. Especially his back.

Ross said something under his breath and turned to meet her gaze. He reached for her. She stumbled against him. Seconds later his lips found hers. His kiss was hungry, igniting something long dormant in her. Her arms reached around his neck and pulled him tight. She would have crawled up him if she could. She couldn't get close enough.

They were two hurting souls who carried secrets that had found release by sharing with each other.

Ross teased the seam of her mouth and she opened to him. Her tongue greeted his like a long-lost friend. His danced and played with hers until her center throbbed with need.

"Sweet Sally," Ross whispered against her jaw as he kissed his way up to nibble at her ear. She shivered. "I always want you to touch me. Please touch me."

How could she resist such a tempting invitation? Her fingers found the hem of his shirt and she ran her hands upward over his chest. It was as firm with muscles as she remembered. The little brushing of hair was soft and springy. Her hands traveled to his waist then on to his back.

"It feels so good to be touched by you. I've dreamed of this too many nights." Ross kissed behind her ear.

He'd been dreaming of her? Her heart picked up a beat. She brought his mouth back to hers and kissed him with all the desire that had been building for days. He was the kindest, most caring and charming man she knew. A hero in every way.

While she kissed him, his hand pulled at her shirt. Lifting it, he drew it off and dropped it to the floor as his mouth floated over the top of one of her breasts. She shuddered from the pleasure. He stepped back and looked at her for a moment. "So perfect."

Ross lifted a breast as his head bent and his wet, warm mouth slipped over her nipple. The throbbing in her core pounded as her blood ran red hot. He slowly sucked and worshipped first one breast then the other. She closed her eyes, absorbing the pleasure of having Ross touch her as she ran her hands through his hair, savoring every tantalizing movement of his tongue. She'd found another of his talents.

When Ross broke the contact, she sighed in disappointment. He gave her an intense look, desire blisteringly strong in his eyes. Swinging her into his arms, he carried her to the bed and laid her gently on it. "I want you, Sweet Sally. I desire you with everything in me. What happens between us is up to you. You have the control."

She opened her arms to him.

"Say it, Sally. Say you want me. I need to hear it."

Her gaze met his. "How could I not want you, Ross? Of course I want you. Please."

He tugged his borrowed sweatpants off her, leaving her bare to him. She grabbed for the sheet but his hand stopped her.

"No, I want to see you in the morning light. You're so amazing."

He studied her with such intensity that she blushed all over. Sally looked away but not before she saw the length of Ross's manhood pushing against the front of his shorts. He desired her. After learning she wasn't enough for

Wade, it was exhilarating to see visual evidence of Ross's need for *her*.

"This is unfair. You need to take your clothes off." She almost whined.

There was a swish of material and her eyes jerked back to him. His manhood was even more impressive without covering. Ross put a knee on the bed as if he were coming down to her.

She placed a hand on his chest. "Shirt too. I want to touch, see you."

"But…"

Her heart went out to him, but she wouldn't let him think he wasn't good enough in every way. "Ross, I trusted you and you need to trust me."

His face showed pain seconds before he murmured. "Others have been disgusted."

She rose so that she could cup his face. Turning it back to her, she gave him a long kiss. "I'm not those others. You're more than your scars to me."

His earnest eyes found hers. "I want you too badly. I can't take the chance."

"Sit down." She patted the bed beside her. He stepped back, looking hesitant. She sat up, trying to appear more assured than she felt, especially since she was naked in the daylight in front of Ross. She needed him to decide what the next move would be.

Slowly, Ross sat next to her. She kissed his arm at his shoulder. "I want to see. After this first time, it won't matter ever again between us. I want to admire all of you. I don't want just part of you."

Moments passed. Finally, he removed his shirt in one quick jerky motion. He put his elbows on his knees.

She didn't look at his back right away. Instead she ran her hand lightly across his shoulders. He flinched but settled. Her fingers gently touched each dip and pucker. "Such strong shoulders. You have to remember I've seen what they're capable of. Felt them hold me."

Some of the tension in him eased away.

Sally looked at his back. Covering one entire shoulder blade were wrinkled, reddish marks and twisted skin. She drew in a breath, not from the ugliness of the sight but from the horror of the pain Ross must have experienced. Moisture filled her eyes. Her heart broke for him.

Ross moved to stand. Her fingers wrapped his biceps, stopping him as she laid her head against his arm. "I'm so sorry you had to go through that. It must've hurt beyond words."

He eased back to the bed but there was still stiffness in his body.

Sally moved so she was on her knees behind him. She placed her lips on his damaged skin. Ross hissed. His skin rippled.

"You don't want to do that." His voice was gruff.

How had other women acted when they saw him? What had they said to this amazing man to make him feel so unworthy, ashamed of himself? Her tears fell. Didn't he know how special he was? She placed her hands on his shoulder, keeping him in place. She gently kissed the scarred area, then worked her way to the nape of his neck.

She wrapped her arms under his, pressing her breasts against his bare back. Her hands traveled over his chest as she continued to kiss him. First the back of his ear, then his cheek. Her hands dipped lower, to tease his belly button, then to brush his hard length.

With a growl that came from deep within

his throat, Ross twisted and grabbed her, flipping her to the bed. His mouth found hers in a fiery kiss.

Ross's length throbbed to the beat of his racing heart. When had a woman made him feel so wanted, needed? Undamaged? Ross couldn't get enough of Sally. Of her tenderness, concern, her compassion. It had taken his breath away when she had kissed his scars. As if she had peeled away all the hurt associated with them. No one had ever understood what it had been like for him as a boy or a man to carry those scars. Until Sally. She had cried for him. He'd seen her eyes.

He would make it his mission to give her all the pleasure she deserved, in and out of bed. Her breasts had been silky against his back when she had pressed against him. It had been years since he'd allowed a woman to see his deformity, to remove his shirt. To know all of him, even the broken parts. The wonder of being so close heightened his desire for Sally.

He cupped her breast and swept his thumb across her nipple until it rose and stiffened. His mouth surrounded it, his tongue swirling. Sally moaned and lifted her hips against him.

"Easy, Sweet Sally, we've all day, if you wish."

He left her breast to place a kiss on her shoulder blade. Her hands flexed on his back in a begging motion. His lips took hers as his hand glided over her waist, along her hip to her thigh. It circled to the inside of it, then returned to her hip. He was rewarded by her legs parting in invitation.

Ross accepted it. His hand fluttered near her heat. Asking, then begging, before he ran a finger over her opening.

The purring sound that came from Sally increased his hunger to a consuming need.

He dipped his finger into her hot center. She squirmed. Slipping it in completely, he then pulled it out. Sally trembled. Her tongue, entwined with his, mimicked the movement of his finger. Lifting her hips, she pushed toward him. Holding her tight, he entered her again and increased the pace. She arched against him, her body tensing before she broke their kiss and eased to the bed. Her eyes drifted closed on a soft sigh.

Ross was gratified by her pleasure. But he wanted to give her more. She deserved it. He rose over her and kissed her deeply. Her arms circled his neck. She returned his kisses with her own. Her lips went to his cheek, his temple, to his neck, then down to his chest. Her hands ran over him with abandon. When they went to his shoulders, he faltered, but Sally didn't slow her movements. He forgot his apprehension and concentrated his thoughts on the feel of Sally's hands touching him, bringing him closer.

Ross captured her hands and gave her a gentle kiss before he rolled away from her. Fumbling with his bedside-table drawer, he located the package he was looking for. He looked down at Sally. She looked beautiful and bereft at the same time. Opening the package, he covered himself. His gaze met hers. "Are you sure?"

"Oh, yes, I'm sure." She drew him back to her.

Ross settled between her legs. His tip rested just outside her heat. Supporting himself on his forearms, he leaned down to give her a long slow kiss. Slowly he entered her. And with a final push he found home.

He almost pulled out completely before he drove into her again. His mouth continued to cover hers. Sally lifted her hips to his, meeting and matching his rhythm until they created their own special tempo. She quivered as her fingers dug into his back. He pushed harder, his pleasure growing.

On a cry of ecstasy, Sally stiffened and relaxed against the bed. He groaned and followed her into a joyous oblivion he'd never known before.

Ross woke to the sound of water running in the bathroom. Sally came into the room, wearing her own clothes. Apparently, she'd gone looking for them in the dryer. Her hair was pulled back and damp strands framed her face. His chest expanded with pride. She had the looked of a woman recently fulfilled.

"You're awake."

He frowned as she didn't meet his eyes. He didn't want any uncomfortable moments between them. He smiled. "I am, but I missed you when I woke."

She blinked. "You did?"

"I did." Ross sat up. "You could've woken me. I would've liked that."

Sally gave him a perplexed look. "Really?"

They watched each other for a moment.

What was she thinking? Had he said something wrong? "Yeah. Who wouldn't want you beside them?"

The worried look across her features disappeared, then she smiled. "Thank you. That's not what I'm used to. My ex-husband didn't like for me to linger in bed. He always wanted me to get up and get a shower."

Ross wanted to hit something. "Look at me, Sally."

She did.

Hopefully she could see the sincerity in his eyes. "You're welcome to stay in bed with me as long as you want or you're free to leave whenever you want. It's up to you. I want you to understand this next part. It's very important that you do." He paused. "I promise I'm nothing like your ex-husband. I don't, nor will I ever, control your actions. You can always trust me, and I'll always be honest with you. Inside and outside of bed."

"Oh."

"Yes, oh. And by the way, right now, I'd like to have your sweet lips on mine but if that isn't what you want, then that's fine."

Her eyes opened and closed a couple of times

before a smile came to her lips. She came to him. Placing her hands on his shoulders, she leaned down. Her kiss was hot and suggestive, setting him on fire again. When he tugged her toward the mattress, she stepped away.

Looking down at him, she teased, "Hey, I need some food if I'm going to keep up with you."

"Okay, let me get a shower and I'll take you out to eat." Ross flipped the sheet back. He didn't miss the sparkle of interest in her eyes as she looked at him.

"Uh...you don't have to do that. I'll see what I can find in the kitchen." She stepped toward the door.

Ross headed toward the bathroom, chuckling. "Good luck with that."

It wasn't until the water was running over him that he realized that he'd been completely naked in front of another person without being self-conscious. And Sally's look had been an admiring one. What miracle had she performed on him?

Done with his shower, he found Sally busy in the kitchen. "I see you found something. It smells wonderful." He walked up behind her, giving her a kiss on the neck. "What're you fixing?"

"I found enough for an omelet and some toast. That work for you?"

"It does. As usual, I'm impressed. Your cooking is one of the many things I like about you." He turned her to give her a proper kiss. "What can I do to help?"

"How about getting a couple of plates for me and setting the table while I finish up these eggs?"

He did as she requested. She plated an omelet and started on another. He took the bread out of the toaster and added it to the plates. She carried those to the table while he filled her glass with water and poured himself a cup of coffee. At the table, Ross sat beside her instead of across from her. He wanted her within touching distance.

They ate for a few minutes, then Sally said, "I called about my car. It's going to be Monday or Tuesday before they can get to it. I know you've a lot of things to do around here so I hate to ask you to take me home." She looked away from him. "But I'd really rather not have

Kody come get me. He'd ask a bunch of questions I don't want to answer."

Ross understood that. Kody was protective, even making his position clear to Ross. He didn't want the third degree from him either. "Do you have any plans for today?"

Sally shook her head. "No, other than I'd planned to sleep and not open a book."

"You could do that here, if you want. I'll be glad to run you home, but I first need to check on a few things around here after the storm."

"Do you mind if I help?" She leaned forward as if eager to do so.

The women he knew were generally more interested in their fingernails than doing manual labor. He couldn't keep his surprise out of his voice. "Sure, if you want."

"If you don't want me to…"

He reached across the table and took her hand. "I'll take any help I can get, anytime, especially if it's yours."

That put a smile on her face.

"I need to see about Romeo and Juliet. They need to be let out into the pasture. Then we need to check the fence—since I did the work in the dark there may be more repairs. Next is the tree. You sure you're in for all that?"

"I'm sure." Sally smiled as she cut off a bite of omelet and forked it into her mouth.

After eating, they cleaned up the table and kitchen together. With that done they once again pulled on the high boots and headed outside.

"Horses first." Sally walked beside him toward the barn.

"Yep." They took a few more steps before Ross asked, "Do you mind telling me about your ex-husband?"

She was quiet for a moment. Ross feared he might be ruining things between them, but he needed to know about the man who had clearly done Sally so much hurt.

"There's not much to tell. We were only married for a little over a year. He was the Mr. It in our part of the world. The football quarterback from a prominent family, the good-looking guy, the one with the best car. Why he looked at me, I have no idea."

"I know why. Because you're great," Ross assured her. She was an amazing person. Why wouldn't she recognize that?

"Thanks. That's always nice to hear but harder to believe after being married to Wade."

"Based on what you said earlier I'm guessing your ex was pretty controlling." Ross glanced at her, measuring her reaction to his statement.

"It turns out he was. I didn't realize it at first. Maybe it was there all along and I just didn't want to see it. I was already working as an EMT when we married. I have always dreamed of being a doctor. Wade knew that, but he didn't want me to go to school. I gave it up for him. It turns out that he didn't give up anything for me. Including his girlfriends."

Ross stopped short and looked at her. "What're you talking about?"

"Kody didn't tell you?"

"Tell me what?" For those who knew him well, they'd have recognized his ominous tone.

"Wade ran around on me. He started about six months into our marriage. I tried to make it work. Crying, begging, counseling—nothing worked."

Ross blurted a harsh word before bringing her into a hug. "You deserved better than that. It's a good thing he doesn't live in town or I'd beat him to a pulp with my bare hands."

She gave him a watery grin and started walking again. "That's close to what Kody said. I guess I just wasn't enough for Wade."

"Enough?" Ross followed her. He couldn't believe what he was hearing.

"Of course you were, and still are. You're *more* than he deserved." He gave her a look he hoped showed her just how sexy and desirable she was. "I should know."

They entered the barn.

Her smile was appreciative, but her eyes still said she didn't totally believe him. "Kody encouraged me to move out here because he didn't want me facing people every day who knew the truth. At first, I wasn't brave enough to make the move, then I decided I had to."

Ross cupped her face. "You're brave in every way I can think of."

"That's nice of you to say."

Ross lifted her chin with a finger. "Hey, I'm not being nice. I'm telling you the truth."

Putting her hands flat on his chest, she backed him against the wooden stall gate and kissed him with a passion he'd only dreamed of. His hand slipped under her shirt and found the warm skin there. Her finger curled into his jean loops and brought his hips tightly against her. His body became rocket hot. He was going to have her right here on the barn floor.

Only the whinny and nuzzle of a horse's nose against his head brought Ross back to reality. He and Sally chuckled and patted Juliet.

"She must be jealous." Sally grinned.

"Or just hungry," Ross quipped as he opened the stall door and brought the horse out. He ran his hand over her coat and looked at her legs.

"Is anything wrong?" Sally asked, standing nearby.

"Nope. Just making sure she didn't get hurt in the storm." He then let the horse wander out of the barn into the pasture. He gave Romeo the same care before letting him go. "Now to the fun stuff."

They went to the shed, collected his tools and headed for the fence.

"You want to do fence work again? Worse, stack wood?" Ross still couldn't believe Sally was choosing to do that type of work.

"Sure. You could use the help, couldn't you?"

"It would be nice to have." And it would.

She shrugged. "I'm a captive audience."

"I can take you home first." Ross was really

hoping she would stay. He enjoyed her company. Sally looked unsure for a moment. Did she think he wanted her to leave? "Hey, you're welcome here for as long as you want. I'm glad to have you anytime."

Her expression eased. "I like it here. I just don't want to overstay my welcome."

He stepped to her and took the tips of her fingers in his, not daring to bring her any closer for fear he'd never get the work done. "That could never happen. Stay all day..." his voice lowered "...all night too."

She looked at him and gave him a soft smile. "I'd like that."

His heart soared. "Then it's settled. Now, let's get to work. When we get the fence and tree taken care of, I'll cook you the best steak you've ever eaten and show you the stars."

That put a teasing smile on her face. "You're cooking?"

He tapped the end of her nose. "You just wait and see."

Over the next few hours they worked together making the fence stronger and cleaning up the limb that had fallen. Ross couldn't have asked for better help. Sally seemed to know what he needed done before he had to ask.

"You've done this kind of work before," Ross stated as he stacked firewood from the truck at the back of the house.

"More than once. My father believes that every woman needs to be prepared for what comes along. Kody and I were expected to help out the same."

"Smart father."

She smiled. "I think so. For me to do things like this used to drive my ex-husband crazy. His idea of work was to call someone on the phone."

Ross had heard enough about her lousy husband. He didn't want to hear any more. "You're welcome to do as much or as little as you want. I'm happy for the company."

She looked off toward the grazing horses in the pasture. "This is such a great place. How could you not like working on it?"

"I feel the same way." Ross threw the last log on the pile. "Let's clean up and go pick out our steaks."

"I was thinking, since I have limited clothes

and these are dirty again, I'd stay here and take a nap and let you pick mine out."

He walked into her personal space and looked into her face, flushed from vigorous activity. "You trust me that much?"

"And more."

Ross raised a brow. "More?"

"Sure. Let's see, I've seen you run into a burning building and save a man's life, watched you care for your niece and nephew, and you saved me when my car broke down. You're a hero. All you're missing is a cape. I think I can trust you with a steak."

He swaggered his shoulders. "Put that way, I do sound pretty impressive. But you forgot one thing."

Her brows grew together in thought. "What's that?"

"How good I am in bed."

Sally's cheeks turned pink. "That goes without saying."

Male satisfaction swirled through him and he leaned into the heat of her. "It does, does it?"

She slapped at his arm. "Don't get too full of yourself. Now you're fishing for compliments."

Ross wrapped an arm around her waist

and pulled her tight against him, kissing her soundly. He wiggled his eyebrows wickedly. "I'm even better in the shower. Want to find out?"

Hours later Sally stretched like a cat in the summer sun. The sound of Ross's truck returning had woken her from a nap on the swing. She smiled. He was right, he did have talents under running water. They'd made love in the shower and then on the bed before he'd dressed and left for the store. Made love? Was she falling in love?

She sat up. What was she doing playing house with Ross? She had plans that didn't include him. She'd temporarily lost her mind. But she couldn't deny that she liked being around him. He was fun, interesting, exciting. All the things she'd been missing in her life for too long. Just seeing his smile made her happy.

No, she wouldn't go down that road anytime soon. She had her life planned out and she wasn't going to deviate, not even for someone as wonderful as Ross. But why couldn't they be friends? Enjoy each other's company for a while? After all, it had only been a couple of days. What she had to do was see that things between them stayed fun and easy. Nothing messy. She'd had messy and wasn't going there again.

Sally stood to meet Ross. He stepped out of the truck with both hands full of grocery bags. He was so handsome that it almost took her breath. What made him even more appealing was that he had no idea of how incredible he was.

His smile was bright and sincere. He appeared as glad to see her as she was him. She liked that. Now she could see that her husband had never looked that way when he'd returned to her.

"Hey, sleepyhead, I can see you've been hard at it."

She leaned against the porch rail. "You told me to take it easy."

He started up the steps. "I didn't say that."

"That's what I heard."

Ross chuckled. The sound was rough but flowed like satin over her nerves. That was him. Metal on the outside and cotton on the inside.

"You need help?" She reached for the bags.

"Not with these but there's a couple more bags in the truck." He gave her a quick kiss.

Sally held the door open for him, then went to the truck. She returned with two more bags and a bundle of flowers.

Ross was unwrapping a steak from white butcher paper when she joined him. "The flowers are beautiful."

"I thought you might like them."

She narrowed her eyes at him but grinned. "Are you romancing me, Ross Lawson?"

He gave her a kiss. "Would it be all right if I were?"

Her heart skipped a beat. She loved the concept but she had to make sure things didn't get too serious. "You do know that for both of our sakes we have to keep this uncomplicated?"

"I do, but that doesn't mean I can't give a friend flowers, does it?" He pulled out a couple of baking potatoes then a loaf of bread from one of the bags.

When he put it that way it was hard to argue with him. "Can I help you do anything?"

He continued to sort items. "Nope. Tonight's your night off. I'm gonna cook for you, if you don't mind?"

"I don't mind at all." In fact, it was sweet of him. She wasn't used to people doing things for her.

Ross turned on the oven and put the potatoes in. "It'll be about an hour before it's ready. You're welcome to keep me company or go back out to the swing."

"Do you mind if I pick out some music?"

"No, as long as it's country and western." He gathered some spices.

"That figures." She went to his stereo beneath the TV and found a radio station. "I'm going to at least set the table."

"Okay. And do you mind seeing to the flowers? They're *not* my thing."

Ross prepared them a lovely meal that included flowers in the center of the table. While they ate, they talked about music, movies and TV shows they liked.

It was just what Sally needed, relaxed and enjoyable. Ross was good company. Why didn't he already have a special someone? "Have you ever been married?"

His head jerked up from where he'd been cutting his steak. "That came out of the blue."

She lifted a shoulder and let it drop. "You're

such a good guy I was just wondering why you aren't taken."

"I think there was a compliment in there somewhere but, to answer your question, I was engaged once."

Somehow it hurt her that he'd had someone he'd cared enough about to ask to marry him. "You were?"

He nodded. "Alice. She's a local Realtor."

Sally knew who she was. "She's the one with her picture on the billboard."

"Yep, that's the one."

Sally stopped eating and rested her chin on her palm, watching him. "So what happened?"

He put down his fork and knife. "It turns out she hated my job. And my scars were a constant reminder of the danger. After a while she just said she couldn't do it anymore. To make her happy I was going to have to give up being a fireman, and that I couldn't do. She couldn't get past her fear, so we broke it off."

"I'm sorry, Ross." She understood the pain of knowing you weren't what the person you loved wanted.

"I have to admit it took me a while to get over

her, but we would've been miserable. I could've never made her happy. I know that now."

Sally reached across the table and squeezed his hand.

They finished their meal and cleaned up.

When the last dish was put away, Ross said, "Dessert will be under the stars. It'll be dark soon. I have a few things to get together. While I do that, would you look in my closet and find something to keep you warm and bring me that sweatshirt hanging on the chair in my room? I'll meet you at the truck."

She did as he asked and was waiting beside the truck when he came out of the house with a basket in hand. Under his other arm was a large bundle. He put both in the back of the truck.

He held the door open for her. "Hop in."

Ross turned the truck around and started down the drive. He drove about halfway and stopped, turned off the truck and got out, leaving the door open. "Stay put. I'll be right back."

She leaned out the door. "Is something wrong?"

"Nope. This is where we were going."

She laughed as she watched him through the rear window. He climbed into the truck bed and unrolled the bundle. With it flat, he returned to the cab and plugged a cord into the electrical outlet. Seconds later an air mattress started to fill.

The pump was so loud she couldn't question him until the mattress was full. She called out the door once more, "Hey, Captain Lawson, this is starting to get a little kinky."

He came to the door and gave her a suggestive grin while he removed the cord. "Normally, I would've driven out into the pasture but with the storm last night it's too wet. So I'm improvising. Give me a few more minutes and I'll have everything ready. Don't look."

It was hard but she did as he asked.

Moments later he returned and offered her his hand. "Okay, come with me." He guided her around to the end of the truck. The tailgate was down. There was a sleeping bag spread out over the air mattress and another lay along the tailgate, making a cushion. Off to the side was the basket.

"What's all this?"

"Dessert under the stars like I promised." Ross looked proud of himself.

"Looks nice." She was impressed with the

thought he'd put into doing something nice for her. Sally smiled at him. "I'm not sure about your plans for that mattress."

"Have you ever lain on a metal bed of a truck?"

"No."

He grinned. "Trust me, you'll like the mattress better."

His hands went to her waist and he lifted her to sit on the tailgate. He joined her, then reached for the basket. "Would you like a beer?"

"Sure."

He opened the basket and gave her a long-necked bottle with a Texas Star on the label.

Sally took a swallow. "It's good."

"I have a friend who microbrews this." Ross took a long draw on his before he reached into the basket again and pulled out a prepackaged chocolate cake with a filling. He offered it to her. "Dessert?"

A laugh bubbled out of her. She took it. "My favorite. Thanks."

He pulled his own out. "I aim to please."

They ate while swinging their legs, occasionally intertwining them as they watched the sun set. When the stars started to pop out, Ross put their empty bottles in the basket along with their trash.

"It's time to climb on the mattress. You go first, otherwise we might bounce the other one over the side."

Sally giggled and scrambled onto the mattress. When Ross joined her, she floated up, then down as if she were on a trampoline as he settled beside her. He pulled the sleeping bag they had been sitting on over them.

"Come here." Ross reached for her. She settled her head on his shoulder.

Over the next hour they lay there huddled in their own cocoon of warmth and silence watching the black sky fill with sparkling stars that looked like diamonds thrown across velvet. It was the most perfect hour of her life. One that she didn't dare hope to repeat.

Ross rolled toward her. His hand slipped under her shirt and traveled over her stomach as his mouth found hers. They made love beneath the stars.

She was wrong. It was the most perfect night of her life. So perfect Sally was sorry it couldn't last forever.

CHAPTER SEVEN

ROSS GLANCED AT Sally as he pulled into the auto-repair place Monday afternoon. The last couple of days together had been wonderful, but it had to stop. What was going on between them was surely nothing more than hot sex between two ambitious workaholics. She would be going back to work tomorrow. Him the next day. One day soon they'd be sharing the same shift. What then? He wasn't that good of an actor.

For them to date, or whatever they were doing, was against department policy even if they did somehow find time for it. Sally was bent on becoming a doctor. He had the promotion to think about and nothing could get in the way of that. If the word got out…

They hadn't said much on the ride in. It was as if Sally was working through what the last few days had meant just as he was. Could she be as uncertain of what was developing between them as he?

After pulling into a parking spot, he turned off the truck and took a moment to gather his thoughts, then looked at Sally. Her attention seemed focused on something out the front windshield.

"Sally—"

"Ross—"

They both gave each other weak smiles.

"You go first," Ross said.

"I'm not sure how this is supposed to go. I've not been in this position before." Her words were slow and measured.

This didn't sound like something he wanted to hear. But he couldn't disagree with her.

"Ross, I had a wonderful weekend."

Now he was sure it wasn't something he wanted to hear. "Why do I think there's a 'but' coming?"

She shrugged. "Because there is. I think we need to chalk this up to just that, a nice weekend. We need to just be friends."

"Ugh, that's the worst thing a woman can say to a man." Still, he couldn't argue with the wisdom of what she was saying.

Sally touched his hand for a moment, then withdrew it. "I really like you. But I can't be distracted from what I'm working toward."

"I'm a distraction?" He rather liked that idea.

She offered him a real grin then. "Yeah, you're a big distraction. I just think we need to stop this before it gets out at the house, or we get too involved. I don't have time in my life for this...whatever it is. It was a great weekend. Let's leave it at that."

Now she was starting to talk in circles. Yet those were the same thoughts spinning in his head.

She continued. "I think all we'd be doing is complicating each other's lives."

That was an understatement. She'd already gotten further under his skin than any woman since Alice. Yet being in a relationship with a person he worked with could only mean disaster.

"Besides that, I promised myself after my divorce I wouldn't be sidetracked from what I want ever again."

That statement didn't sit well with him. He didn't want her to change her dreams for him.

"You think I want you to give up what you want?"

"No, I just think I'd eventually do it for you. I have before."

Ross didn't like that statement any better, but he could understand it. "I want to be Chief one day. Us seeing each other could be a problem. A big one."

She waved her hand. "See, that's just what I'm talking about. It makes sense that we just remain friends, no more. It would make life too complicated for us to date."

"I think you're right." So why did it seem so wrong? He reached and took her hand. "Good friends."

She squeezed his hand. "Very good friends."

"May this friend give his best friend one more kiss before she goes?" Could he survive if she said no?

She gave him a sad smile. "I'd like that. You're a fine man, Ross."

"You're really sweet, Sally."

He brought her to him and gave her a kiss that quickly turned from friendly to hot.

Sally broke away. "See you around, Ross." She opened the door and was gone.

Why did he feel as if he'd just agreed to something he might regret?

The next few days were long. He missed Sally. Wanted to see her, talk to her, touch her. Even being at his place didn't feel the same. He went into work for the first time with little enthusiasm simply because she wouldn't be there. He didn't like this arrangement and he was going to tell her so. There must be another way.

As soon as his shift was over, he would go to her place and talk to her. See if she felt the same.

Ross was walking in the direction of his truck the next day at the end of his shift, just after noon, when Kody called his name. He turned.

"Hey, man, you want to play some hoops for an hour or so? I don't have to pick up Lucy until three."

"No, not today. I've got something I need to take care of."

Like convincing your sister to come back to my bed.

"Well, okay. Talk to you later."

"Yeah." Ross climbed into his truck. Kody was a hurdle he'd have to face one day soon.

Maybe he and Sally could keep their relationship from him and the department until it fizzled out, which it surely would. In the meantime, he wasn't ready to give up on Sally. Hopefully, she was of the same mind-set.

Ross pulled up in front of her apartment building ten minutes later. The work crew had moved on to the next building but they still made it difficult to find a parking place. Sitting with his hands on the steering wheel, Ross studied Sally's front door. What was he going to do if she wasn't home? Worse, if she didn't want to talk to him? He hated to appear desperate to see her, but he was. What if she rejected him? He'd been dodging that emotion for years. It didn't matter. He needed to see her, talk to her. Tell her how he felt.

Climbing out of the truck, he walked to the door with determination. He raised his hand to knock and lost his nerve for a moment. Then he knocked.

Sally had done most of the talking last time. Now he was going to do it. Maybe he could change her mind. He wasn't going to know until he tried.

He didn't hear any movement. Fear she wasn't

home swamped him. He thought of returning to his truck, but then the latch moved. Moments later the door opened. Sally's questioning expression quickly turned to one of pure joy.

It filled him too. He smiled and opened his arms.

She squealed and jumped into them. Hers circled his neck. He chuckled, stepped inside and kicked the door closed with the heel of his shoe. She rained kisses over his face as he backed her against the wall.

"I know we shouldn't be doing this but I missed you." Desperation filled her voice.

He chortled with pleasure. "I guessed that." His mouth took hers in a hot, hungry kiss. She could have missed him only half as much as he'd missed her. It was heaven to have her body against his again.

"What're you doing here?" Sally asked between breathless kisses.

"I wanted to talk to you."

She pulled at his shirt. "Is that all you wanted?"

"Hell, no," he growled, returning his mouth to hers as he worked at the snap of her pants.

* * *

Sally had been longing for Ross, but hadn't known how much until she'd seen him in her doorway. Her heart had almost flown out of her chest with excitement. Her neighbors would have thought she had lost her mind if they had seen her acting like a kid at Christmas.

As she and Ross lay in bed, she scattered kisses on top of his chest as her hand roamed his middle.

She was in trouble. Once again she'd gone over the line into the land where her heart was becoming involved. The problem was she didn't know how to step back to safe ground. What she had to guard against now was making the mistake of changing what she wanted for Ross.

He groaned. "You keep that up and you'll get more than you bargained for."

She shifted so she could see his face. "Who said I didn't want more?"

Ross smiled indulgently down at her. "Mmm… That's the kind of thing I like to hear." He leaned in to kiss her.

"Ross, what're we going to do?"

The look in his eyes turned devious. "You don't know by now?"

She gave him a little pinch. "You know what I mean. We agreed to be friends."

"You don't think I'm being friendly?" His hand traveled over her bare butt.

"You're just not going to listen, are you?" Her voice held a teasing note.

Ross kissed her neck. "Who said I wasn't listening? I heard every word you've said."

"Ross, we can't do this."

"I think we did 'this' just fine. Great, in fact." His lips traveled lower.

"We have to stick to the plan." Her voice had turned sharper than she had intended.

He captured her gaze. "Look, why can't we just enjoy each other while it lasts? We don't have to make a big deal of it. We can keep it between us. We can be friends and still see each other when our schedules allow."

"I guess that'll work." She wasn't convinced. The more she saw Ross, the harder it became to give him up. Hopefully, one day soon she would have medical school to think about. There wouldn't be any time for a relationship. But she'd miss him desperately if she gave him up right now. Maybe if they just saw each other until she started school…

Over the next few weeks she and Ross fell into a routine. If they both had extended days off, then Sally would go to his place. They would work around the ranch, go out for dinner in a small town nearby. They couldn't afford being seen together by someone in the fire department, so they made sure to stay out of Austin. When their schedules had them working back-to-back days, then Ross would come to her apartment. She'd never been happier. Or more worried about her heart being broken.

It was exciting to know Ross would be waiting on her when she came home or be coming to her after his shift. Against her better judgment, she was caring for him a little more each time they were together. Still, one day soon it would all have to end, but that wasn't today.

Sally was leaving his place to go to work when Ross said, "I promised Jared and Olivia when they got out of school, I'd take them tubing on the Guadalupe River. We're going Saturday. Wanna come?"

"I wish I could, but I told Kody I'd watch Lucy. He's scheduled to work. He's started asking me what I'm doing with my time. I haven't seen much of either of them since you've been keeping me busy." Her look was pointed, yet she grinned.

"And I like keeping you busy." His smile grew. "Lucy's welcome to go. I know Jared and Olivia would have a better time with her along."

Sally's heart lightened. She would've missed seeing Ross. Her feelings for him were like trying to stop a runaway train. She was doing everything she'd promised herself she wouldn't do. "I'll talk to Kody and ask Lucy and let you know."

"That sounds like a plan. I'll get the tubes together."

"Can I do something?"

"No. I think I can take care of the sandwiches for lunch. All you have to do is get you and Lucy here in your bathing suits." He came in close, moving to stand between her legs where she sat on his kitchen counter. "I especially like that idea."

She grinned. "I thought you might." Then she kissed him.

Kody gave his okay that also included a suspicious look when she told him Jared and Olivia had requested that she and Lucy came tubing with them and Ross.

"You've lived here for over a year and had nothing to do with Ross Lawson. Yet in the last month or so you've spent the day with him at the picnic, watched his niece and nephew, studied at his house and now you're going tubing with him. Is something going on I should know about?"

"There's nothing going on. We're just friends. Aren't I allowed to have friends?"

"Yeah," he said, but gave her a narrow-eyed look implying he was unconvinced.

Early Saturday morning Sally picked up Lucy. This time Sally was the one the most excited about going to Ross's. She hadn't seen him in a couple of days because he had worked a double shift. He'd worked his regular shift, then gone to the Fire Department Office for a meeting the next day. There was something off in her day when she didn't get to see him.

She didn't know how much longer they would be able to keep their relationship a secret. It was getting more difficult every day. Sometime soon they'd have to work together. In fact, she was going to get to find out sooner rather than later how good of an actor and actress they were because the new schedule had come out the day before and they were to share a couple of shifts next week.

What then? Would someone notice the looks between them? Or that one knew more than they should about something the other did on their days off? It would be so easy to slip up. It could damage Ross's career and she didn't want that.

He deserved the Battalion Chief position. As a dedicated firefighter, a great leader and someone who had a vision for the future of the department, he was a perfect fit. More than that, he had a passion for fighting fire. It wasn't just a job to him. Ross completely believed in what he was doing.

As she and Lucy traveled closer to Ross's house, Sally's heart beat faster in anticipation. She smiled to herself. This was what happy felt like. It had been a long time since she'd been that. She'd counted on medical school to give her that feeling again. Then along had come Ross.

He and the kids were waiting on them beside

his truck. He wore a T-shirt and swim-trunks along with a pair of tennis shoes. There was a ball cap on his head and his eyes were covered by aviator sunglasses. He had never looked better. She banked the urge to run into his arms, reminding herself to remain cool in front of the kids.

Lucy started waving before Sally stopped the car. The kids returned it, and Ross offered one as well.

He was at her door before she opened it. Was he as happy to see her as she was him? As she climbed out, he stepped toward her. Sally had no doubt he planned to kiss her. His intent was obvious. She stopped his movement with a hand to his chest and a dip of her head toward Lucy. Ross looked past her shoulder. With the sag of his shoulders and dimming of his smile, he nodded and backed away. Lucy would no doubt enjoy telling her father the moment she saw him again that Ross had been kissing her aunt Sally. She certainly wasn't prepared to field Kody's questions about that.

In an odd way, sharing a clandestine relationship with Ross was exciting. Fun like she hadn't had in a long time. She didn't have to share him with anyone. Yet some part of her wanted people to know this amazing man belonged to her. But did he?

"Come into the house. I've got to put our lunch into a dry bag, then we'll be ready to go." Ross started up the porch steps.

"Dry bag?" Sally followed him.

"It'll keep things dry. I'll tie it to my tube." He held the door for her.

"Great idea." She went inside.

"I'm full of those." He called over his shoulder, "Kids, we'll be right out. Make sure you've got your towels and anything else you need in the truck."

As soon as they were inside out of sight of the kids, he hauled her to him and kissed her. There was hunger there, yet tenderness as well. He'd missed her too. "I'm not sure how I'm gonna make it all day without touching you. With you just being an arm's length away."

Sally giggled. She seemed to do that often lately. It was empowering to her bruised self-image to be considered so desirable by such a remarkable male. Ross made her feel as if she was enough. That was something Wade hadn't done, ever.

Ross pursed his lip in thought. "Maybe it was a bad idea to invite you along."

She pulled away, pouting. "I could always get Lucy and leave."

"Over my dead body." Ross pulled her back to him. She liked being against him. "I'll take my chances on having you around. I'll just have to work on my self-control today."

"That's more like it. You're just gonna have to restrain yourself, because I can promise you that Lucy will catch on pretty quick. I don't think either one of us wants to face Kody quite yet."

"I can handle Kody. You and I are adults. Now, how about one more quick kiss for the road?" Ross's lips found hers.

Too soon for Sally they went to the kitchen. Ross already had the sandwiches in individual plastic bags. He placed them in a heavy rubberized bag. "Do you have anything you want to put in here?"

"My phone?"

He carefully put the food in the bag. "I'll take mine, so why don't you leave yours in the truck?"

"Okay. I don't guess we need two of them."

"Roger that."

Ross locked up, and they joined the kids at the truck. The tubes were already loaded and secured by straps.

"Climb in, kids. Buckle up," Ross called.

They scrambled onto the back seat. Sally climbed into the passenger's seat and Ross got behind the wheel. The kids chattered for the hour it took to drive to the river. Ross pulled into the makeshift dirt parking lot.

When the kids climbed out, Ross put his hand over hers. "I'm sorry we didn't have a chance to talk, catch up."

She smiled at him. "I don't mind. I'm just happy to be with you."

He gave her a bright smile. "That was certainly the right answer."

"Come on, Uncle Ross. Let's get on the river," Jared called with impatience.

Ross unloaded the tubes, handing one to each of the kids then her. After passing out the life vests, he took a moment to secure the bag to his tube. "Okay, kids, huddle up."

The three of them circled in front of him. Sally joined them.

"What're the rules on the river?" Ross gave

them an earnest look. He was such a good leader. He would one day make an excellent head of the fire department.

"Stay together," Olivia said.

"Wear your life jacket at all times," Jared added.

"Then we'll have fun," Ross finished. "Got it?"

In unison, they all said, "Yeah!"

He led the way to the riverbank. She helped the kids put on their life vests and get into their tubes and soon they were all floating down the river. The day was warm and the water cool. They leisurely rode the current, letting it take them at its speed. The kids laughed and splashed each other, then turned on her and Ross. A few times other people or groups passed them.

Once the kids were ahead of them enough that Ross came up close to her. His look remained passive and focused on the kids while the hand closest to her went beneath the water.

She jumped as his hand ran over her bottom. "Oomph."

"Easy," he said in an innocent voice. "You don't want to make a scene in front of the kids."

As he said this, one of his fingers dipped under the leg opening of her bathing suit and worked its way around to the crease of her leg before it was gone. That was all it took for her center to start throbbing. With a teasing smile on his lips, he floated away.

"Not fair, Lawson."

He gave her a wicked grin over his shoulder.

Not much farther along, Ross called a halt, telling the kids to pull over to the sandbar where the water was placid. It was time for lunch. They brought their tubes out of the water and found a log to sit on. Sally pulled the sandwiches, health bars and bottled water out of the bag along with napkins and a small package of wet wipes. Ross had thought of everything.

It didn't take the kids long to eat. Soon they were asking to go swimming.

"You can go but stay close to the shore," Ross told them.

She and Ross watched as they headed for the water.

"This tube floating is fun. I've never done it before. I'm really glad I came. Obviously, this isn't the first time you've gone." Sally looked at Ross and bit into her sandwich.

"It was a regular pastime when I was growing up. Jared and Olivia have been a few times before."

"This won't be my last time either." With or without Ross, she intended to do this again. The only thing was that when she did, she'd always think of Ross. It would take some of the joy out of it.

"I'm glad you're having a good time." His attention remained on the kids.

Again, the thought he'd make a good father entered her head. And the fact that such a thing would never involve her left her a little sad. Shaking it off, she sighed. "There's nothing more refreshing than a day on the river when it's hot."

"I can think of at least one other thing." Ross's suggestive remark was accompanied by a heated look. Placing his palms on the log, he leaned back.

Sally took a swallow of water, set the bottle down in front of the log, then leaned back in the same manner as him. She placed her hand over Ross's, intertwining their fingers. Ross looked at her and smiled before his attention returned to watching the kids.

"I'm going to miss you tonight," Ross said in a mock whisper.

Sally tried to act unaffected, but her heart was already picking up speed. "You think so?"

His eyes flickered with burning need as he looked at her. "I know so. Lean over here. I want to kiss you."

"The kids—"

He glanced at them. "Aren't looking."

Her lips met him for a quick kiss.

With a sigh, Ross called, "Let's go, kids. Come clean up your trash and put it in the bag. We have to carry everything out we bring on the river. Then get your tubes."

Within minutes they were back on the water.

They had been floating for about an hour when they reached a bend in the river and heard, "Help, help, help."

In seconds Ross was off his tube. He shoved it toward her and started swimming. As he passed the kids, he ordered, "Stay with Sally."

He disappeared around the bend as she and the kids picked up their pace. As they rounded the curve, she could see Ross stepping out of the water at a calmer area up ahead. She directed the kids that way.

When they reached the spot where Ross had exited, she told the kids in a stern voice, "We're getting out here. I want you to pile your tubes here beside the river and go over there to that spot and sit." She pointed at a log. "Do not take your life preservers off. Stay put while I see if your uncle Ross needs my help. I'm trusting you to do as I say."

Ross was kneeling over by a woman lying on the ground in a small grassy area. There was another woman sitting on the ground beside her. Sally hurried to them.

"What's wrong?" she asked, coming up beside Ross.

Ross shifted and she could see that the woman had a compound fracture just above her knee.

"How did this happen?" Sally asked.

Ross said to the women, "This is Sally. She's a paramedic. She'll help you."

"We got out of the river to look at a flower and stupid me got my foot caught in a hole and fell," the injured woman said between tight white lips.

Ross could handle burning buildings or automobile wrecks, but he wasn't good at physical emergencies. He had EMT skills, which he rarely used. The woman had severely broken her leg and he was more than happy to turn her care over to Sally's excellent knowledge.

He went to where the kids sat. As he reassured them, Ross searched the dry bag for his phone. Finding it, he punched in 911 then returned to Sally, who was talking to the injured woman.

"I've got 911 on the phone. What do I need to tell them?"

"Thirty-four-year-old female," Sally stated in a firm voice. She was clearly in paramedic mode. He relayed the message. "Compound fracture of the right femur. Treating for shock."

Sally already had the woman lying down with her uninjured leg up.

"Heart rate steady. Pulse one-twenty. Moderate pain. Splinting now."

Ross repeated everything to the dispatcher. He said to Sally, "A medivac can't get in here. The tree canopy is too heavy. We'll need to get her downriver to the takeout spot. It's about a mile away."

Sally spoke to the injured woman's friend.

"Please see if you can find at least three pieces of wood or straight sticks that can be used as splints. They must be sturdy." As the woman moved away, Sally asked him with worry in her voice, "What's the plan?"

"I'm going to lash the tubes together and float her down. We're too far from the road for the ambulance, and the helicopter can't get in here."

Sally nodded. "Okay, I'll have her ready. Have one of the kids bring me the towels. I've got to manage shock if we're going to do this."

"I'll get started on the raft now." He hoped it went as smoothly as he had it planned. Ross went to the kids and issued orders for them to hunt for long sticks but to stay within eyesight of him. He sent the towels by Jared to Sally.

Pulling four of the tubes close to the river, Ross put them side by side. Without thinking twice, he jerked his T-shirt over his head. He then pulled a knife out of the dry bag and cut and tore the shirt into strips. He glanced at Sally to find her struggling to do the same with her shirt. Ross went to her. Taking the shirt out of her hands, he began tearing it as well.

"Thanks," Sally said.

He pointed. "I'm going to need one of those towels."

"Okay. I'll put my life jacket over her."

"You can have mine as well." He took it off. "I'll need any of your leftover strips."

The woman's friend came back with some sticks. Sally's attention returned to splinting the woman's leg.

The kids had found some sticks. Some he could use, others not. He sent Jared back out to look for more and had the girls hold things in place as he tied the tubes together with the strips of his shirt. He then tied the sticks on to give the woman a platform to ride on.

The whop-whop of the helicopter flying in could be heard in the distance.

"You ready, Sally?"

"Ten-four."

"Okay, kids, we're going to get this lady on the raft. Then I want you to each get in your tube. I'm going to tie you to the raft. Sally and I'll be swimming. Understand?"

The kids spoke their agreement.

"Stay here until we get the woman settled," he told the kids and then joined Sally.

She had the woman's leg secured in a splint of branches and strips of T-shirt. The leg was evenly supported on the bottom and the top. Sally had made sure it wouldn't move.

He spoke to her. "I've been thinking about the best way to move her. I could pick her up while you support her leg."

"I can help," the woman's friend said.

Sally looked down at the woman. "I don't see that we have a choice." She then said to the injured woman, "What happens next isn't going to be fun. Hang in there and we'll have you at the hospital in no time." She smiled. "And on pain medicine."

The woman nodded, her mouth tight. "That sounds good."

Sally turned her attention to the friend. "Take the towels and life jackets to the raft. Lay one towel over the sticks. We'll cover her with the others again."

The woman did as Sally instructed and removed a towel and the life jacket lying over the injured woman and hurried off.

She soon returned, and she and Sally helped Ross get the injured woman into his arms by supporting her hips and legs. His thigh muscles burned as he strained to lift her. She cried out in pain but there wasn't anything they could do for her except be as gentle as possible. That he was already trying to do. It was a slow process walking over the rough ground, but they finally made it to the raft. Ross placed her on it. Sally quickly checked to make sure the woman's life jacket was still secure. She then covered the patient with the towels and her and Ross's jackets.

"Let's get the raft in the water," he said to the woman, then, "Kids, get your tubes."

It took the three adults to lift and scoot the raft out until it floated not to jostle the woman.

"Sally, will you take one of the front corners? You." He spoke to the friend. "Will you take the other? I'll take the back. Kids, get on your tubes. I'll tie you on."

Everyone did as he instructed. "Okay, let's get this show on the river."

Slowly they moved out into the current.

"I'm looking for slow and steady," Ross called. "No sudden moves."

It took them almost an hour to get to where the helicopter was waiting on the slow winding section of the river. As they came into sight, the medivac crew went into action. They had a gurney and supplies waiting at the river edge when they arrived. Sally gave a report while he saw to the kids.

As they watched the helicopter lift off, Sally said, "I'm glad you were there with me on this one."

His fingers tangled with hers for a moment. "I was just thinking the same thing about you."

She smiled up at him. "You do know you aren't wearing a shirt, don't you?"

"Yeah."

"You okay with that?" Sally gave him a concerned look.

"I'm a little antsy, but handling it."

Her fingers found his again. "I'm proud of you."

Ross squeezed her hand, then let it go. "Couldn't have done it without you."

"Oh, yeah, you could. I've no doubt you would've done whatever was necessary to get that woman to safety whether or not I had come along. That's just the kind of guy you are, Ross Lawson. You're made of hero material. Scars and all."

When Sally thought he was a hero, he felt like one.

"Thanks, you were pretty heroic back there too."

She laughed. "Now that we've told ourselves we're wonderful, how about let's go home?"

Ross laughed. "Let's go."

They gathered the kids and caught the next shuttle back to the truck. The other floaters riding with them asked questions about the incident and offered their appreciation for a job well done.

At the truck Ross turned to the kids and said, "I think we've all earned pizza and ice cream. Who would agree?"

The kids cheered. Sally smiled.

"Okay, I'll order in and stop and buy the ice cream. Since we don't have enough clothes on to get out anywhere."

It wasn't until then that he registered he'd not given a thought to riding the shuttle or being around the kids without a shirt on. They hadn't even noticed. Maybe he made more of a deal of his scars than they were. There was something freeing about that knowledge.

The kids climbed in the back seat of the truck. Ross hadn't driven far when he looked in the rearview mirror to find them all asleep.

"Hey," he whispered to Sally.

She looked at him. He nodded toward the back seat. "Don't you think you're too far away?"

Sally glanced behind her and grinned before she slid over against him. He put his arm around her shoulders and pulled her close. She kissed his cheek. "You were my hero again today. The raft was brilliant."

Ross kissed the top of her head. "No more than you."

He glanced at Sally. What had happened to him in the last few weeks? He'd changed. Sally had made all the difference.

CHAPTER EIGHT

SALLY PULLED INTO the fire station parking lot two days later with a grin on her face. She was going to see Ross. Her smile grew as she remembered how unhappy she'd been at the idea of seeing him just weeks before. It had been four days since she'd truly been in his arms and she missed him terribly. She could understand where his ex-girlfriend had been coming from about odd schedules. Working around them was difficult but she would never give Ross up just because of that.

The day was coming soon when she would have to. But even as she thought it, she wondered if she did have to give him up. Couldn't they work something out? Did she want to? It was already happening. She wanted to make changes in her life to accommodate Ross. But if she did, could she trust he would always be there for her? His job was important to him.

If it came down to her or his job, he'd take his job every time, wouldn't he?

When she entered med school—make that *if* she entered med school, as she still hadn't heard back from her test—she could only imagine how difficult it would be to make time for a relationship. Would they be together that long? No, she wouldn't let things get that far. At the beginning, she wouldn't have thought she and Ross would have lasted this long but now she couldn't imagine not having him in her life. For now, she'd just have to enjoy the time they did have while it lasted.

There had been a particularly sad look in Ross's eyes when she and Lucy had left his house after they had gone tubing. It was nice to have a man so disappointed to see her go. To show it so honestly. After her husband's betrayal, her self-esteem had suffered greatly. Ross's attention had gone a long way in restoring it.

The day they'd tubed the plan had been for Lucy to stay the night with her, so Ross couldn't come over that evening. Kody had asked her to join him and Lucy for supper the next evening.

All of this made it seem like an eternity since she'd had personal time with Ross.

She was beginning to believe they might have something special. She'd never felt this way before. That low-level hum of need for Ross was always there. That jump of excitement when she saw him always thrilled her. The anticipation of his touch made the prospect of seeing him more rousing.

Now she was thinking in circles. Not making sense. One minute she was thinking of when their time together would end and the next she was dreaming of a future with Ross. She had to stop thinking with her heart and focus on what her mind was telling her or she was going to get hurt, badly.

It had become tedious, even nerve-racking to keep their relationship to themselves. She was tired of it. Two grown people had every right to see one another. She wasn't ashamed of Ross and she didn't think he was ashamed of her. At least letting Kody and Lucy in on her and Ross's secret would help.

She pulled her bag out of the back seat of her car and headed into the station. Inside the engine bay, she turned toward the paramedic side of the building. She saw Ross on the other side with his hands in his pants pockets talking to one of the firefighters. He glanced her way. Even from that distance she could see the glimmer of awareness in his eyes. His body language changed, as if he wanted to drop what he was doing to come to her. Her heart did a skip and a jump.

Sally entered the paramedic supply room and walked on into the locker room to put her bag away. She sensed more than saw someone enter behind her. Glancing behind her, she found Ross. He stood with his back to the door, blocking it. If anyone tried to enter, they couldn't unless they pushed him out of the way.

"Ross, what're you doing?"

"Come here." The words were low and forceful.

She narrowed her eyes. This wasn't like him. "What?"

"Please come here, Sally." His voice was solemn but had a pleading note, as if he physically hurt.

That warm spot in the center of her chest that grew when she was around him heated. Now she understood. She walked into his arms.

Ross's hands cupped her butt and he pulled her up against him as his mouth found hers. His searing kiss was sensual and stimulating, leaving her in no doubt where his mind was.

Ross soon set her at arm's length. "I keep that up and everybody'll see what being around you does to me."

She giggled.

He grinned. "You like that idea, don't you?"

"It does have its appeal." She gave him a nudge. "Now, Casanova, move out of the way and let me see if the coast is clear." He stepped to the side. She opened the door and looked out. "You're good to go, Captain Lawson."

As he went by her, she brushed his cheek with her lips.

The shift was a busy one. There were no fires but a number of auto accidents. One of them required the Hazmat team. Ross was especially trained for Hazmat so his crew was out cleaning up past the end of the shift. Sally didn't see him before she left. They hadn't discussed their plans, so she decided to go home. Disappointment washed over her as she drove out of the parking lot.

It was early evening when she settled down to read her mail. She still hadn't heard from Ross. She suspected he'd had a large amount of paperwork to do but she would've thought he'd have called or texted by now.

There was a knock at the door. Her heart started racing with hope.

Ross stood on her stoop. He didn't say a word. Just scooped her into a hug and kissed her. Her soul went wild with joy. She clung to him, wrapping her legs around his hips.

"Happy to see me?" He sounded pleased.

He pushed the door closed with his foot, held her with one arm and locked the door. Starting down the hall, he continued to kiss her as he found her bedroom. There he rolled them onto the bed with a bounce.

Sometime later, still in bed, they snacked on popcorn and watched a comedy show.

Ross fed her some corn. "After our shift I know the definition of hell. It's having you so close yet being unable to touch you."

Sally giggled. "I kind of like the idea. It's flattering."

"That may be so, but it's not much fun for me." He kissed the corner of her mouth.

"You can touch me all you want to right now." She gave him a suggestive smile.

His hand skimmed the inside of her thigh. "Now, that sounds like an excellent idea."

Ross started his shift two days later feeling rather good about himself. He looked out of his office window to see Sally standing beside the ambulance talking to her crew member. She glanced over her shoulder and made eye contact with him.

Heat washed through him. He was acting like a lovesick male horse that hung its head over the fence hoping the female horse in the next pasture would notice him.

Focus, Lawson. You have that promotion on the line.

He attempted to turn his attention to his paperwork. Instead his mind went to memories of his last few days off. A short while after the comedy show had ended, Sally had accompanied him home and they'd spent the time at his place. She seemed to thrive there. Which gave him a warm feeling deep inside that he didn't wish to analyze. She was becoming ingrained in his life, as necessary as the air he breathed.

He not only appreciated her body, he enjoyed being with Sally. She had a sharp wit that kept him on his toes. She thought nothing of working right next to him, even when the job included mucking out the barn. She was game for anything. More than that, she made him feel like the hero she said he was. Not once had he seen her flinch when he removed his shirt, which he'd started doing regularly when he worked on the farm. She treated him as if he were whole and flawless. With her, he was.

They didn't talk about the future. Ross worried if they did it would change things between them. He didn't want that. Giving up Sally would already be far harder than he had originally thought. He'd ride this wave of happiness for as long as it lasted. It was too wonderful to let go of.

Sally was a partner both outside of work and at work as well. Today, she'd be sharing the shift with him, then they would have another few days together. For him life was good. The only thing that could make it perfect would be to earn the Battalion Chief position. Hopefully he'd know about that any day now, after his interview a week ago.

The company made a few runs during the early evening but managed to have dinner in peace. He and Sally sat next to each other around the large table with the rest of the people at the station. They made an effort to appear as normal as possible, yet under the table he slid his foot next to hers and Sally pressed her lower leg against his.

The alarm beeped and the dispatcher came on over the intercom just after sunrise the next day. Rush hour almost always meant an accident and this one was no different. Ross hurried to the bay and suited up with his crew. He climbed into the truck and the driver flipped on the lights and siren.

Ross swung into emergency mode, already thinking through the possibilities of what was ahead for him and his firefighters. Dispatch told him it was a four-car accident. His team had to work their way through and around the traffic. The ambulance was right behind them.

As they arrived, Ross assessed the situation. Apparently, a car turning left in the intersection ran into the side of an oncoming car. The other two cars had hit their rears. The car that had been going straight took the worse of the crash. Gas covered the ground. A few people sat on the curb off to the left.

Ross was on the radio issuing orders before he climbed out of the truck.

"We need fire extinguishers out just in case. Make sure that gas doesn't spread. Don't let the medics in there until we know how many we have involved and the area is secure." He wouldn't put anyone in danger, especially Sally.

The ambulance pulled up next to his truck with the help of the police directing other cars out of the way. One of his firefighters led a woman to the ambulance. Sally took care of her while the other EMT checked on those on the curb.

"Are all the people in the cars accounted for?" he asked into the radio.

"Ten-four," one of his firefighters came back.

Ross's attention returned to the scene. His firefighters had the situation in hand. He glanced at the box to see Sally taking care of a man who looked as if he was in his thirties.

Into his radio he said, "Let's get traffic moving and clean up this mess."

"Ten-four," came back from his men.

Ross directed the wrecker into place, then

started toward Sally, who had a different patient sitting on the back bumper of the box now. She stood in front of the man, tending his head wound.

The man started to stand, but Sally put a hand on his shoulder and eased him back down. In a flash her patient slung his hands high, one of his fists hitting Sally in the face. Her feet came off the ground and she landed on her butt.

Ross roared her name. Something inside him that he didn't recognize roiled to life. Bile rose in his throat. Raw heat flashed over him.

He ran toward Sally. Reaching the man, Ross curled his hands into his shirt. He didn't think—just reacted. Jerking him around and away from Sally, he lifted the scumbag to his toes and shook him. How dared he touch Sally?

Ross growled with fury. "You sure as hell better not have hurt her."

"Stop, Ross! Stop!" Sally's voice penetrated his anger. Her hands pulled at one of his arms.

The policeman took the moment to capture an arm of the man and Ross let go. Seconds later, the policeman had the man's hands secured behind his back.

"What're you doing?" Sally demanded in a

loud voice despite the fact she stood in his personal space.

"Helping you!" Ross's heart pounded as if he'd been in a race for his life. The man had knocked Sally to the ground. She could have been seriously hurt.

Sally glared at him. "I could've handled him."

Ross studied her, making sure she had no major injuries, then ground out, "Yeah, I can see that by the shiner you're going to have."

Sally's partner joined them. "He's right. You took a hard shot. You're going to need to be seen at the hospital."

Sally shook her head. "I'll be fine."

"Do as you're told, Sally," Ross snapped and stalked off. Didn't she understand she could have really been hurt? His heart had constricted when she'd gone down.

Ross had been shocked at how quickly he'd reacted to Sally being hit. He was known for his calm demeanor and even thinking during an emergency. Emotions didn't enter into his decisions—ever. But where Sally was concerned, he stepped out of his norm.

His heart still slammed against his chest as he walked back to his post. Slowly he calmed down. Started thinking straight, but the damage was already done.

Sally had only been doing her job. Surely she'd been pushed and hit before by a crazy patient. The difference was it hadn't happened in front of him. Something primal had fueled him. He was going to protect his woman. In seconds, he'd shifted into defensive mode.

One of the firefighters handed him his radio. Ross hadn't even realized he'd dropped it. His lieutenant gave him an odd look when Ross joined him. Ross didn't acknowledge it. Instead he started issuing orders.

Who had seen his over-the-top reaction? Would they put two and two together and figure out he and Sally were seeing each other? Worse, would his loss of professionalism get back to the bosses?

Sally went to the hospital emergency room against her will even though she knew it was necessary. It was company and fire department protocol that it be done. Thankfully, X-rays indicated there were no broken bones, but she had to admit her face throbbed. It had already started turning dreadful colors just as Ross had said.

She'd been told not to return to the station. Someone had been called in to replace her. A policeman had given her a ride home.

Ross had broken their professional relationship. In two. She could've handled the situation. He had overstepped his bounds. His reaction had been way over the top. She'd never seen him act that way. Part of her appreciated him caring enough that he was that concerned about her, but it wasn't good for either one of their careers for him to go ballistic, particularly where she was concerned. It was just an example of why they should not be seeing each other. What if the higher-ups got wind of what happened? It might hurt Ross's record.

Yet she kind of liked the idea he'd ridden to her rescue. Chivalry wasn't dead. Once again, he was her knight in shining armor.

There was a knock at the front door. That would be Kody. She'd called him and asked if he and Lucy could come over for the night. She had to have someone with her. With a bag of frozen peas over her eye, she opened the door. Instead of Kody and Lucy, Ross walked in without invitation, carrying a white bag. She watched, bewildered, as he made his way toward the kitchen.

"Hey, you do know I'm mad at you?" she called to his back.

He glanced at her with concern on his face. "Are you all right?"

She followed him to the kitchen. "You know I am. You called twice while I was in the ER. All I have is a black eye. I'm under a concussion watch for the next twelve hours because of the bump on the back of my head, but I'm fine. About your behavior..."

In one swift move he put the bag on the table, turned to her and grabbed her shoulders, looking deeply into her eyes. "Let me make this clear right now. For the rest of my life whenever I see somebody hit you, I'll react the same way. No apologies." He pulled her to him and held her as if she were a new duckling. Tender, but reassuringly safe.

Had he been that scared for her?

Finally, he released a deep breath and let her go. "Have you eaten?"

"No."

"Great. I brought us Chinese takeout." He started removing small white cartons out of a bag.

Just like that they were moving on.

"You need to put those peas on that eye. It looks painful. By the way, why doesn't a paramedic have a disposable ice pack in her own apartment?"

"I'm not a paramedic *all* the time," she said in a huff.

He took her hand and kissed the palm. "I know that. I even like it. A lot." He kissed her and she returned it. "It hurts me to know you were hurt."

This type of attention she could learn to love. In fact, Ross would be easy to love. She was halfway there anyway. Her chest felt heavy. This was just what she'd been afraid would happen. Could she go back? Pretend those feelings didn't exist? Ross coming along wasn't part of her grand plan. "I'm all right, Ross. The guy was on drugs. Those people are always unpredictable. Next time I'll have a policeman secure their hands before I see about them."

"Next time? There better not be another one where you get hurt." He hugged her again. "For somebody who has dedicated their life to caring for people like you have, then have somebody do you that way..."

She cupped his face. "You do know it comes with the territory sometimes."

"Yeah, but that doesn't mean I have to like it." He suddenly looked tired. As if his emotions had gotten the best of him.

"Says the man who runs into burning buildings." She could well remember how she had felt when he had run into the burning house.

"Let's eat before it gets cold."

It was as if Ross couldn't stand to talk about what had happened anymore. As if his emotions were too open, fresh. She'd focused on her feelings and not enough on his. Ross was being so sweet she couldn't be mad at him anymore. He really had been scared.

They had just finished their meal when there was a knock at the door.

"That'll be Kody."

Before she could get up, Ross rose and went to the door. "I'll get it."

How was Kody going to react when he saw Ross at her place? He'd already started asking questions.

"Come on in. She's in here," she heard Ross say.

Lucy came down the hall. Ross and Kody were still at the door. What were they saying to each other?

"Aunt Sally, are you okay?" Lucy asked, making it impossible to hear the men.

"I'll be fine. You don't need to worry about me." Sally patted the cushion beside her.

Lucy plopped down.

A minute later Kody, flanked by Ross, came into the living room.

"So how're you doing, Sweet Pea?" Kody stood above her, studying her.

"A black eye and a bump on the head, but I'm fine. I should be good by tomorrow."

Kody dropped his bag with a thump. "So…" he glanced at Ross, then focused on Sally "…we're here to watch over you."

"That won't be necessary," Ross said from where he leaned against the wall. "I'll be here." His wooden tone implied his mind wouldn't be changed.

Sally's heart tapped as she looked between the two men.

Kody's head whipped around in Ross's direction. "Really?"

"Yes." Ross didn't miss a beat as he gave Kody a steady look. These were two bulls marking their territory of protection.

Abruptly Kody looked at her. "So it's like that?"

Sally nodded.

Kody looked at Ross, who flatly said, "It is."

Sally watched her brother's face harden. "I'm sorry to have bothered you. I didn't know Ross was coming when I called you."

"Lucy, honey, there's been a change in plans. We won't be staying tonight." Kody waved her toward him.

"But I wanted to stay," Lucy whined.

Sally put her arm around Lucy's shoulders. "When I'm feeling better you can come back."

Ross walked Kody and Lucy to the front door. Sally listened from where she was.

"Lucy, go wait in the truck. I'll be right out," Kody told her. The child obediently went. Sally held her breath.

"You break her heart and I'll break you."

Ross returned with a firm "Ten-four."

CHAPTER NINE

Ross stood next to the fire engine two days later, working on his monthly equipment inspection, when he noticed the Battalion Chief's truck pulling into the station parking lot. It was Battalion Chief Marks.

He and Chief Marks had been friends for some time. Ross had been in his company when he'd first joined the fire department. Chief Marks had been a mentor to him, even encouraged Ross to put in for the Battalion Chief position. What made this particular visit interesting was that he wasn't Battalion Chief over Ross's station. Was this good news or bad news?

Anxiety filled Ross. Did Chief Marks have news about the selection?

"Hey, it's nice to see you." Ross walked toward him with a hand extended as his friend entered the station.

"Ross." Chief Marks shook Ross's hand.

"How's Jenna and the kids?" Ross asked.

"Doing great."

"Good. What brings you over to my side of town?"

Chief Marks's expression turned serious. "I wanted to talk to you about something that has come up."

"That sounds ominous," Ross said a little more casually than he felt.

"Why don't we go into your office to talk?"

"Okay." Ross led the way. In his office, he dropped his clipboard on the desk and sat in the seat behind it. Chief Marks took the chair across from him. "So what's up?"

"I'm not going to beat around the bush on this, Ross. I heard something happened the other day during a run that had to do with a female paramedic."

Ross didn't try acting as if he didn't know what Chief Marks was talking about. "I was just taking care of my company."

Chief Marks's look held steady. "You sure there wasn't more to it?"

Ross knew there was more to it. However, what he was having trouble determining was just what "more to it" meant. He wasn't going to lie. That would come back to haunt him. This man was his friend. Had his best interests at heart. "Yeah, we're seeing each other."

Chief Marks leaned back in his chair, crossed his fingers over his belly and pursed his lips.

Ross returned his direct look. Sally had been upset with him. Apparently, she'd been right, if the Battalion Chief's question was any indication. It might have been unprofessional for him to have grabbed the man, but Ross was a human first and he had been scared for Sally. Seeing her hit had made him roaring mad. He'd be that way again where she was concerned. That was the problem. He couldn't ignore his feelings for her. Now he had to deal with the fallout of his actions.

"I'm going to shoot you straight here. This isn't good for your promotion. I don't think the Chief has heard about it, which is in your favor. Only time will tell on that. If he does, it very well may be the end of your chances for Battalion Chief. I'd hate to see that. You're a good firefighter. Are you in love with her?"

Was he? Ross wasn't sure. He did care—a lot. His performance the other day proved how much he cared. But love? That meant forever for him. He'd been concentrating so hard on not examining his feelings that he wasn't sure. "I think I am."

"Then I suggest you think things through carefully. What you decide may mean your career." Chief Marks stood.

Ross did as well.

"I hope I get to see you in the Battalion Chiefs' meeting soon." With that, Chief Marks left.

In his own way, he had told Ross what he should do. But could he?

He and Sally had started as a fling, a weekend together. Then it had stretched to a few weeks. Yet as the days went by he wanted more. She seemed to as well. They'd not spoken of ending things in weeks. Now that the time had come he didn't want to. What he felt for Sally was real. Something special. He couldn't just throw it away. They needed to find a way to make this work. Wasn't there some design where he could have both? He couldn't just walk away from her.

He desperately wanted that Battalion Chief job. He'd worked all his professional life to earn this promotion. He'd done the schooling, taken the additional classes and been the best captain he could be. The only hiccup had been this period with Sally. Why should the Battalion Chief position hang on his personal life? If he got the job and didn't have Sally, what would he really have? When had she become the most important? It didn't matter, just that she was.

The problem would niggle at him until Ross spoke to her. Surely together they could work something out where they could both have what they wanted. She would return to work the next day, but he had to talk to her before then. They couldn't share another shift until they'd had the conversation. He called her and she agreed to meet him at his place instead of him going to hers.

Ross didn't remember the drive home. All he could think about was the upcoming discussion. He needed a solution. Sally would be going to medical school soon, of that he had no doubt, and that would improve the situation greatly. If she'd moved, then they wouldn't be working together even between semesters.

His chest tightened. What if she didn't care as much as he did? They'd never spoken of their feelings. He had to jerk the truck back to his side of the road before he was hit. Was he planning for something that didn't even exist? A fling was their agreement. Now he was wanting to change that. There had been no promises between them. What if she didn't want any? He and Alice had made promises and nothing had come from them—what if that happened again with Sally? Panic started to build. Suddenly the promotion seemed a small concern.

When Ross arrived home, Sally was waiting on the porch swing. He would always think of her that way. She loved the swing. It was her favorite place. His heart quickened. Sally was nice to come home to.

She came to the top of the steps and waited. He took her into his arms, kissing her with all the care he felt. She returned his kiss with equal enthusiasm.

Afterward she giggled. "I see that Texas star is still working for you."

"Yeah, and I'm going to use it every chance I can get." He kissed her again.

She reached for his bag. "Let me have that and I'll put it up while you go see to the horses."

He let her take the bag. Their talk would come soon enough.

* * *

Sally found Ross under the large oak tree a few minutes later. He stood beside the fence looking off into the horizon.

"Hey." She placed her hand between his shoulder blades and rubbed his back. "Something bothering you? How were things at the house today? Anything exciting happen?"

He didn't answer immediately while his attention remained on something out in the pasture. "Chief Marks came to see me."

She grabbed his arm. What did that mean? Had Ross gotten the Battalion Chief position? She wanted it for him so badly. She knew it meant as much to him as her doing well on the MCAT did to her. Excitement bubbled in her. "He did? Is it good news?"

Ross gave her a sad shake of his head. "Sweet Sally, I hate to disappoint you. No, what he came to tell me was that he'd heard about what happened at the accident the other day."

The colorful balloon of delight at the chance he might have the job deflated with a whoosh. Her stomach tightened.

"He wanted to know if I was seeing you. What the situation was."

She moved away just far enough she could see his face. "And...you said?"

He turned to look at her. "I told him the truth." Ross didn't say anything more for a few moments, then, "He thinks what happened at the accident site could affect my chances for Battalion Chief. The committee looks for any little thing to make a difference between candidates."

Sally bit her top lip. The day had come. "I see."

Ross turned to her. "Sally, help me find some way around this. Together we can come up with a plan. Maybe you could transfer? You're going to school sometime soon anyway. It could be temporary, then you could move back if I make Battalion Chief. I'd be over stations that didn't include Twelves."

She couldn't, wouldn't, be the reason Ross didn't get his dream. That had been done to her by Wade and she wouldn't be the one to do it to Ross. He deserved better. But to transfer? She'd told him once that she wouldn't do that. But what if she did and he didn't get the job? Or she didn't get into med school? She helped Kody with Lucy. If they were in the same station, they could work out the schedule easier. She lived nearby the station house. More than all that, she'd promised herself she'd never re-arrange her life again for a man.

Ross had said nothing about his feelings. What if she upended her life for him? What if Ross never made a real commitment? What if all he wanted was what they had now? She couldn't take chances with her life like that. Too much damage had been done to her dreams and herself by her relationship with Wade and she refused to let that happen between her and Ross.

Sally shook her head. "Ross, I won't be the reason you don't get the job of your dreams. I've been in your spot before. I know what it's like to push your dreams away to make room for someone else's. Please don't ask me to."

He searched her eyes for something she couldn't identify before saying, "We knew all along that this day was coming. One way or another." His voice had become firm, taken on his captain-in-charge tone.

"Yeah, if it wasn't you, it would be me. Hope-fully I'll know something about med school soon. It's been a nice ride while it lasted."

Ross sighed heavily. "It's just that I've worked toward moving up the ranks my entire career. This is my chance. Higher-ranking jobs don't come along often. I believe I can make a difference in Austin's fire department. That I'm the kind of leader they need."

Sally put a hand on his arm. "Hey, you don't have to sell me on the idea. I believe that about you as well. We agreed to keep it between ourselves for just that reason."

Ross was still focused on his job, she could understand that, even hoped the promotion was his, but still it hurt that he wanted it more than he needed her. That even after what she had told him about her marriage, he still had the nerve to ask her to transfer without any mention of his feelings.

But Ross hadn't led her to believe anything different about what he wanted in life. Had never mentioned the future, or wanting more. She shouldn't be upset. If the table was turned, wouldn't she give him up if it meant missing out on med school? She'd let Ross get too close. "This wasn't supposed to be this hard."

He faced her. "No, it wasn't. But we can remain friends."

Sally shook her head. "No, we've tried that before. Coworkers, yes—friends, no. It would never work."

"I guess you're right." His voice was flat.

She looked out at the green pasture with the sun shining across it. Ross's ranch had felt more like home than any place she'd been in a long time. But it had never really been hers. It was a part of that pretend world she'd let herself be drawn into once again.

"I better be going." She went up on her toes and kissed his cheek. His hands came to her waist and he brought her to him. Sally gently pushed him away. "Please don't. It only makes it harder. Please don't come in the house until I'm gone. Have a happy life, Ross."

She held her tears until she reached the front door. In a blurry haze, she gathered her belongings. Stuffing them haphazardly into a bag, she headed out of the house. Ross had honored her request, but he now waited at the bottom of the porch steps.

His lips formed a thin line on his handsome face. Maybe one day he would find the right woman for him, and the timing would be right. The thought made her heart feel as if it were being squeezed to death. If only they were different people.

"Can I help you?"

She shook her head and kept going. He didn't move as she threw her bag into the car, got in and drove away. Yet she was aware that his eyes didn't leave her.

Hours later Ross hit the fence staple another time despite it already being secure in the post. After Sally had left, he'd gathered his fence-repair bag, saddled Romeo and ridden as if the devil were after him to the remotest point of his property. There he'd started checking the fence that was already in good repair.

He was doing anything he could to drown out the voice that poked and prodded that she hadn't been willing to help him find a way around the situation. Hadn't wanted to fight for them.

He didn't like her decision at all, but he really couldn't give a good argument against it. Maybe she was right. Their relationship had been a diversion. If he got the Battalion Chief position, then he would start working on the Assistant Chief position. Yes, this was for the best. If they had waited till later on to break up, it would have just been harder.

So why did he feel as if his heart had been ripped out? Worse, something about the situation made him think he'd treated her far more badly than her husband had.

Maybe when this Battalion Chief stuff was over they could try again.

He shook his head.

No, as long as she was working in the same station as he it would never work. If she didn't get into medical school, she'd have to keep her job. And even if she did, she still wanted to stay on at the station for part-time work. One of them would have to give up something they greatly wanted in order for them to have a relationship.

Ross hit the post even harder.

What they'd had was all there would be.

He jerked his shirt off and used it to mop the sweat off his face. Afterward, he looked at it and groaned. Just a few weeks ago, he wouldn't have even done that. Even when he was alone. Sally had changed his world in more ways than one.

Ross didn't return to the house until just after

dark. He wasn't looking forward to going inside where he'd shared such wonderful moments with Sally. She had permeated every aspect of his life. The thought of climbing in his bed without her drove him to sleep on the sofa.

The next few days weren't much better. Everything in his world had been turned upside down and not for the better. If he'd been miserable before, it came nowhere near the pain he experienced now. What he had to do was learn to live with it.

He hadn't even gotten to the hard part. Working with Sally and knowing he couldn't touch her.

Sally had gone home and flung herself on her bed to sob until there were no more tears.

With Wade it had all been make-believe, and now with Ross… The only difference was that she'd known this was how it would end from the beginning. Still, she couldn't stop her heart from being involved. It was breaking.

Ross hadn't demanded she make changes. He'd suggested it as an idea. She'd known how important the promotion was to him from day one. Ross didn't deserve any comparison to Wade. Had she been putting that on every man she met? Ross had proven trustworthy over and over.

Still, what if she'd been the only one to make concessions and their time together had run its course or Ross had become so caught up in his job their relationship had died? What would she have then? She just couldn't take that chance.

Done with her crying, she climbed into the shower, ordered her thoughts and put her emotions on autopilot before she dressed for work. At least there she would be distracted until she and Ross had to share a shift. That she wasn't looking forward to.

She returned to the station to great fanfare, but her heart was heavy. She put on a brave face, with the intention of not letting on how broken she was. Thankfully everyone was focused on her bright purple eye. It looked worse than it felt. Her heart was far more battered.

Her fellow shift members made fun of her, along with shadowboxing when they walked past her. A couple of them made jokes about Ross's over-the-top reaction to one of his company getting hit. None of them asked any deeper questions about why Ross had acted the way he did. She was glad. Not being honest with them would have bothered her. Talking about him would have made her cry. It would all be out if she let that happen.

She dreaded the day she and Ross shared the same shift. When she'd first become involved with him, she'd known that when they stopped seeing each other their working relationship would be strained. Now they were going to have to deal with just that. It wouldn't be fun, but she would keep moving. She couldn't give up her job just because it was difficult being around Ross.

Her fear came true a week later. The new schedule was posted and there along with Ross's name was hers on the same day. She came to work determined to keep her thoughts on her job and not let the fact she was just feet from Ross for a full twenty-four hours affect her work. She'd have to learn to deal with the reality that she couldn't talk to him on a personal level or touch him on an intimate one. Those thoughts almost caused physical pain. She understood in her head that their being apart was necessary, but her heart wasn't convinced.

Managing to make it to the locker room without running into Ross, she put away her bag. When she returned to the bay, she saw him standing beside one of the trucks talking to the captain of the outgoing shift. She stopped dead still. Her heart drummed against her ribs.

This situation was more excruciating than she'd anticipated. With a fortitude she didn't know she had, she picked up her clipboard and headed for the ambulance to do her routine shift check of the supplies. Ross looked in her direction. She nodded and kept moving. The rest of the shift she stayed on her side of the building. Despite that she was well aware of where he was at all times.

The only time her brain shut him out was when they were on a call. Thankfully it was a relatively busy shift. By the next day and shift-change time, she was more mentally than physically exhausted.

Ross had spoken to her a couple of times to give her directions during a run. There was never anything but professional interaction between them, which was as it should be, yet she longed for more. She'd put a bag of his things that he had kept at her place in the back of his truck before she'd left the station. That was the last of anything personal between them.

The next time they shared a shift, only a few days later, it was better. She kept to herself and had as little interaction with the firefighters as possible. What she feared would happen when she became involved with Ross had. Now she was reaping what she'd sown.

She'd been hurt when she'd found out Wade was cheating on her but none of those feelings compared to what she was experiencing now. It was like walking around as a shell of a person. Ross had become essential to her living and breathing, and not having him was slowly killing her.

She had to get out of this funk. Her grade on the MCAT should arrive any day. When she found out how she'd done, then she could really move forward, make plans. Her focus would be on school and what was happening at the hospital. Still, she would need to do part-time paramedic work to pay the bills and keep her certificate up to date. That would mean working with the fire department and possibly Ross, if he didn't get the Battalion Chief's position.

Somehow she'd get beyond this. Or would she?

It had been a couple weeks since she'd stopped seeing Ross when Kody started asking questions. She was at one of Lucy's school functions when he pulled her off to the side.

"What's going on with you, Sweet Pea?"

She wasn't going to tell him that she was heartsick. "I told you not to call me that."

"Don't evade the question. I know something's going on. You didn't look this bad when you divorced that jerk you married."

"I'm fine. I'm just anxious about my MCAT grades." Or she could tell him she hadn't slept a full night since the last time she was in bed with Ross.

Kody huffed loud enough that a couple of people looked at them. "I was on Ross's shift today."

"What does that have to do with me?" She didn't meet his look.

"It's just interesting that he has the same look."

She said softly, "We're not seeing each other anymore."

Kody bared his teeth. "I told him he'd have to deal with me if he broke your heart."

Sally placed a hand on Kody's arm, giving him a pleading look. "Please don't say anything to Ross. We both agreed it was for the best. His actions when I got my black eye were noticed by the bosses. I don't want him to lose his chances for advancement because of me. I'd never want to be responsible for that. I'm going to medical school, I hope, and I won't have time for a relationship. It's for the best. It's not Ross's fault."

"I just hate to see you hurting."

"I'll get over it."

Kody studied her. "Will you?"

Lucy's program was starting so Sally didn't have a chance to answer. If she said yes, she was afraid she would be lying to him as well as to herself.

CHAPTER TEN

Ross TURNED IN his chair so that he could look out the window into the bay for a chance glimpse of Sally. He did that too often on the days she worked. His time was spent figuring out a way to get through those days in particular and life in general without her. He missed having her as part of his real world. Just seeing her at work wasn't enough. Then again, if he never saw Sally, maybe he'd get over her. Either way, he wasn't sure how to survive. What he was currently doing wasn't working.

Right now, she stood beside the ambulance grinning at her crew member. She hadn't smiled at him in days. Not having her happiness directed at him was a physical hurt in his chest.

Sally kept a low profile, staying on her side of the building as much as possible. The first couple of weeks, that had been fine with him, easier in fact, but now it made him angry, sad. This wasn't a way for either one of them to live. His days had turned tedious and challenging, in not a good way.

The last time they'd worked together he'd scheduled a station meeting that included the medical side before an inspection. He and Sally hadn't been in a room together in weeks. She'd sat in the back keeping as much distance between them as possible. As he'd spoken, a couple of times his glance had met hers. There had been a gloomy aura in her eyes. He'd stammered over his words. It was his fault it was there.

But wasn't it Sally who had agreed they'd just have a good time together? That she wanted no attachment because she didn't want a relationship to interfere with her plans? She'd known what they were doing wouldn't last. So why did she act as if she were taking it so hard? Did she care for him more than she'd let on? More than he'd realized?

At dinner that evening they made sure to sit on opposite ends of the long table where it wasn't easy to interact, yet he was aware of every move she made. Her laugh skated down his spine. It should be him sharing that with her. Something had to give soon. He couldn't continue to live like this.

They were just finishing eating when the alarm sounded. Relief washed over him. Was it wrong of him to be grateful for a call? At least on those he would focus on something other than Sally.

Everyone jumped into action, leaving their plates on the table.

The dispatcher called out: "Three-year-old. Stuck in storm drain. Fifth and Park."

Despite his desire to be elsewhere, this was a call Ross didn't want to hear. A sick feeling filled his stomach. He'd trained for this eventuality, but it was one he'd never been involved in and had never wanted to have to oversee either. He'd heard more than once at seminars that it was the most difficult, emotionally and physically.

To make matters worse, a storm was on the way. And it was getting dark. The clock was ticking on two levels. Could the situation be grimmer?

Ross was out of the truck the second it

stopped at the scene and striding toward the policeman standing beside a sobbing woman.

"What's the situation?" he asked the policeman.

"This woman's child climbed in the drain after a ball and fell in. He's been in there for about ten minutes now. We've heard him crying."

"Ma'am..." Ross placed his hand on her arm briefly, to get her attention "...I need you to talk to him. Tell him someone's coming to get him. Reassure him. Can you do that?"

She nodded.

Ross said into the radio, "I need a blanket over here."

Seconds later one of his firefighters brought it to him.

"Put the blanket down in front of the drain and have the mother talk to the child."

"Yes, sir," the policeman said.

Ross assured the woman, "We'll get him out." As he walked away, he said into the radio, "I need a plan of the drainage lines along here, asap."

"Copy that," his lieutenant replied.

"Have the policeman in charge meet me at the truck," he said into the radio.

"Ten-four. He's right here and on his way," the engineer came back.

Ross talked as he walked, surveying the area. "We're going to need rope, the tripod, and have medical on standby."

"Medical here." Sally's voice came across the air.

At the truck, he told the policeman to see that people stayed back and to reroute traffic. This rescue wasn't going to happen fast.

Ross spoke into the radio. "Remove your turnout gear. Put vests on. We're going to be here for a while. I need three men to meet me at the drain. We've got to get that cement cover off so we can see what's going on." Ross removed his gear. He was wearing a T-shirt, pants and his regular shoes, and added his reflective light coat. He put on a yellow hard hat.

When he joined his firefighters at the drain, the policeman guided the mother away so Ross and the other three men could flip the cover over and out of the way.

"These things are supposed to have a grate," one of the men said.

The policeman offered, "Yeah, but they get missed or rust out. This one doesn't have one for whatever reason and now there's a kid to save."

"Flashlight," Ross said.

Sally handed him hers. He shined it into the hole. It was about twenty feet deep and three feet wide. At the bottom he could just make out the top of a child's head where the drain fed into the larger cross drain. The boy wasn't saying anything now. However, there was an occasional whimper so they knew he was alive.

The problems were mounting. Rain was coming. The sun was setting. The boy was going into shock. Now the narrow drain.

One of the men stated the obvious. "Captain, none of us are small enough to go down."

Could the situation get any more challenging?

"I'll do it." Sally's voice came from behind him.

It could!

She was the slightest on the shift. To punctuate the need to hurry, thunder rolled. Rain would be here soon. The child could drown if they didn't get moving.

Ross's first instinct was to say no, knowing Sally's history. Plus, it was against regulations because Sally wasn't a firefighter, and she hadn't been trained for this situation. But there was no choice. If they didn't move now, the child would certainly die. Ross had to think about the bigger picture. Now that included putting Sally's life in danger.

"Get us some light here. Secure the tripod over the hole. Triple-check the rope and pulley. I'll get Sally into the harness," he told the men. "Sally, come with me."

He led her to the rescue truck. After making sure no one could hear him, he said in a low voice, "Are you sure about this?"

Sally gave him a firm nod. "I'm sure."

"It's everything you hate."

She gave him a determined look. "If I don't go, the child will die."

"We could look for another way." Yet he knew of no other way. He wanted to take this burden away from both of them.

"You and I know there isn't one, so help me with the harness." Her voice indicated she wouldn't discuss it further.

Resigned, Ross pulled the harness out of the

storage box on the side of the truck. He helped her step into it, pulled it into position over her jumpsuit and around her leg before buckling it at her waist. "If I could have it any other way, I would."

She gave him a thin-lipped nod. "I know that."

He took out a helmet with a light on the front, placed it on her head. His gaze met hers as he buckled it under her chin. There was a flicker of fear in her eyes that pulled at his heart. Sally was the bravest woman he'd ever known. She was facing her fears head-on. Could he say that about himself?

"You know, to make this even worse, we're going to have to send you in upside down. The space isn't wide enough for you to turn around to put a harness on the kid. You'll have to go down headfirst, secure him in the basket, come up and we'll pull the kid out. You'll have a headset. I'll be right there with you the whole way."

After what had passed between them over the last few weeks, did that reassure her? Ross hoped it did. He wanted her to trust he was there for her.

"I understand. I can do this."

He grabbed a pair of leather gloves and handed them to her. "These may be a little too large, but they'll be better than nothing."

"Thanks." She pulled them on.

"Okay. Let's go," Ross said.

She called to her crew member to bring the child-size basket. "What's the boy's name?"

Ross asked into his radio, "What's the boy's name?"

"Mikey."

"Ten-four."

When they arrived at the hole, Ross said to Sally, "Don't take any chances. If you think something isn't right, come up."

"Ten-four."

Ross asked one of the firefighters for his radio head unit. He positioned it around Sally's neck. "You don't have to push anything, just talk. I can hear you and you can hear me." He set the channel so that it would only be the two of them on it. Flipping on the light and securing the basket to her chest, he said, "You ready?"

Their eyes held for a moment as the rain started to fall. Sally nodded and he clipped the rope onto the harness. She went down on her hands and knees. As she put her head into the hole, Ross and one of the other firefighters each took hold of one of her legs and guided her in. Another two firefighters manned the rope, slowly letting it out.

Ross's chest tightened to the point he couldn't take a full breath as he watched Sally's feet disappear into the blackness.

Fear clutched her heart as Sally slid into the tight space. The only thing that kept her going was the knowledge that if she didn't do this a child would die. It could have been Lucy, or Jared or Olivia.

By inches, she was lowered. Her head hurt from the blood rushing to it but soon eased as it adjusted. Either way she had to just not think about it. Using her hands, she guided her way down. She was thankful for the helmet light. Without it she wasn't sure she could remain sane.

"Sally, talk to me." It was Ross's deep, calming voice, yet there was still an edge to it. He was afraid for her. Ross knew her fear too well.

"I'm about halfway down. I see the child. He isn't moving."

She continued downward as her clothes began to get wet.

"It's really raining now, isn't it?"

"Ten-four." Ross hadn't even tried to keep his concern out of his voice that time.

"Okay, I've reached him. Hold me here." She hung just above the boy. He was sitting on the mush made of old leaves, grass clippings and garbage with his head leaning against the wall. "Mikey? I'm here to help you."

There was no reply from the child. A chill went through her. She pulled off a glove and used her mouth to hold it. Reaching down, she checked the boy's neck for a pulse. She blew out a sigh of relief. "He's alive, but in shock."

"Ten-four. Now get him in that basket and we'll get you up here."

Water poured in a steady stream around her and over her as she released the basket. It was growing higher in the shaft because the child plugged part of the cross-drain hole. She needed to get the boy out of the way to let water flow into the larger drain before it came above his head. If she could get the basket flat enough to get the child into it, she could move him out into the larger drain long enough for her to go completely down. The water was rising by the minute.

"Sally, talk to me!"

She spat out the glove and took off the other one. They were just in the way now.

"I'm thinking down here!" At least her frustration with Ross's demands was taking her mind off how dangerous all of this was. "Water is getting higher down here."

"We're diverting all we can."

"Lower me another foot." She went down. "Right there."

She needed to lay the basket down beside the boy, but she couldn't have him float away on the water rushing down the larger drain.

"Send the other line down."

Seconds later another rope came down beside her.

"What're you doing?" Ross demanded.

"I'm having to do some repositioning."

"Repositioning?" Ross's voice wasn't as steady as it usually was.

She clipped the line onto the basket, then laid it next to the boy.

Placing her hands under the child's arms, she used all her strength to lift him into the basket. She pulled the blanket in the basket over him the best she could and clipped him in. Water was beginning to wash over him.

"Give me some slack in the second rope."

"Ten-four," Ross came back.

"Now in mine." She went down. "That's good. That's good."

Sally pushed the basket out into the larger cross drain, making sure the boy's head stayed well above the water, then angled the basket against the wall.

"Let me down some more."

"What?" Ross all but screamed in her ear.

"Do it, Ross."

Seconds later she had her head in the larger drain. She was glad to see that it was about five feet wide. Her knees hit the bottom of the small drain. A moment of panic washed through her when she feared her feet wouldn't quite make it but they soon slid down the slick wall. Cold water poured around her. It was rising. Her teeth chattered. She was soon lying on her stomach, with her head raised in the cross drain as water flowed down her sides. Rolling over, she grabbed the boy and pushed the basket back through the opening.

The increasing pressure of the water current made it difficult to maneuver. She braced her feet against the wall to hold her position and held her head up to the point she strained her neck to keep it out of the water.

"Pull him up. Slowly. I can't see him or guide him. I'm having to do it all by feel."

Ross gave the order. The basket started moving. Soon it left her fingertips.

"What've you done? You're supposed to be coming up." Panic filled Ross's voice.

"There was a change in plan. It's a swimming pool down here."

She hoped with everything in her that she could get back into the other drain without any trouble.

"Uh, Ross, it's going to be a little tricky down here for the next few minutes. You mind talking to me and keeping my mind off it while I figure things out?"

"Aw, Sweet Sally, you're killing me. We have the kid. The EMT is checking him right now. He'll be on the way to the hospital soon."

Sally tucked her head back through the hole

into the smaller down drain. So far so good. "How're Romeo and Juliet doing?"

"They're great." His voice lowered. "I think they miss you. I know I do."

If she hadn't been concentrating so hard on what she was doing, she would've reveled in that statement. Sally continued to snake her way upward into the drain.

"Tighten the rope."

Ross gave the order.

"Now pull me slowly. I'm not sure I'm going to make it through this way."

Ross's groan sounded as if he was in agony, then he gave the order.

With the help of the tension on the rope to support her and performing an extreme back bend, she slid through until she was on her knees. She'd have scrapes on her back from that maneuver. Her jumpsuit had been torn. "Stop."

The rope didn't move. She came to her feet. The water came to her calves. She needed to get out of here.

"Is everything all right?" Ross's voice held a note of panic.

"Ten-four. I just needed to stand up." Seconds

later she said, "Hey, Ross, would you mind pulling me out of here?"

He snapped. "Let's get her out, guys."

She was halfway up when she said, "I've missed you too."

"You're going to be the death of me." The words were almost a caress.

Her head had hardly popped out of the hole before Ross's hands were under her arms and she was hoisted against him. "I don't know what I'd do if I lost you."

"Stop, Ross," she whispered, pushing against his shoulders. She looked behind him to see the Battalion Chief watching them. "Don't do this. How do you think it looks?"

Thankfully others grabbed her, so that it looked as if everyone was taking their turn in congratulating her, making Ross's embrace look as if it weren't anything special.

She wiped the dirt on her face as she stood in the heavy rain. To her great amazement Ross dropped his coat, pulled his shirt over his head and started cleaning her face. Embarrassed at his attention, she took it from him and used it to finish the job.

The shirt was soaked yet still warm from

Ross's body. The musky smell of him clung to the fibers. Sally inhaled. It had been so long since she'd been close enough to enjoy his scent. She clung to his shirt.

Someone handed her a blanket. Ross pulled his coat back on.

She winced when someone touched her back.

"Are you hurt?" Ross asked with concern as he pushed people away.

"My back."

He spoke into the radio. "I need a medic over here."

"I've just scraped my back. I'll be fine."

"Maybe so, but you'll be checked out." He handed her off to the paramedic. "Now go."

Ross didn't want to live through anything like the last eight hours ever again in his life. Sally going into the drain had been bad enough but those moments when he'd feared she couldn't get out had almost been more than his heart could take. He'd actually thought he was going to lose her.

He'd been such a self-serving piece of human debris. He'd never once considered Sally's feelings. He'd acted as if it had all been about him, his job. Not once had he questioned if what he was doing was right for them both. He'd encouraged her to have a fling with him when she'd not wanted to out of fear he would act the way he had. Sally had known herself too, known how invested she would become in their relationship.

It hadn't taken him long to learn that she didn't give by half measures, yet he'd pushed her into seeing him when she'd known full well what would happen. The worst part was that he knew her history and had done it anyway. As much as he would like to think that he was better than her ex-husband, he wasn't. He'd treated her the same way. As if her needs and dreams weren't as important as his.

He'd even asked her to make concessions for him. He'd not once considered doing that for her. What kind of person was he? Was he even good enough for Sally? With every fiber in his being he wanted her, loved her. If she would take him back, he'd do everything in his power to be worthy of her.

After they had cleaned up and returned to the house, he'd requested that all the company be allowed to go to the hospital and check on

Sally. They went in as a group. Sally had been asleep most of the time. He was sure that she was exhausted from coming off an adrenaline rush, the cold of the water, the physical exertion she'd endured and the fear she'd had to control. The doctor said she would be fine. She only had bumps, bruises and some major scrapes on her back. They were going to keep her for observation until morning.

"Okay, guys, we need to get back to the house," Ross reluctantly announced. He'd have stayed if he had a choice. Instead he lingered behind the others. Reaching for Sally's hand that lay on the hospital bed, he found it warm, which was reassuring. He kissed her lips before whispering, "I love you."

"Captain..." His lieutenant stopped short at the door.

Ross looked at him as he straightened.

The man grinned. "It's about time you admitted it."

"You knew?"

His lieutenant shrugged. "Heck, we all do."

Ross was shocked. "How?"

The man chuckled. "By the way you look at

her, or don't lately. But the real clue was when you called out her name during the night."

Ross rolled his eyes. "I'm not going to live it down, am I?"

The man squished up his nose and mouth and shook his head. "I doubt it."

With one last look at Sally, Ross left. Tomorrow he'd start eating humble pie and begging her to take him back. Promotion or not, he wasn't giving her up. If she'd have him. He was afraid that would be a huge *if*.

Kody would be caring for her. Ross had called him to tell him what had happened and asked him to take care of Sally until he could get off his shift.

"I thought you weren't seeing each other anymore," Kody said.

"That's going to change."

"It is, is it?" Kody asked with humor in his voice.

"Yes."

"Then I suggest you bring flowers and chocolate because she's going to need convincing. She'll never agree to play second best to anyone or anything else again." Kody's voice held a firm note.

"I know that. I already feel guilty enough without you piling it on. I don't plan for her to ever be second best again. She'll always be the most important to me. She'll come first."

"Then I'd make that clear and keep that promise."

"That's what I plan to do. Now, will you pick her up at the hospital and get her home until I can get there?"

Kody huffed. "Come on, Ross, I've been watching over her all her life. I can handle this."

"After this time, it'll be my job." Ross hung up.

The station had made the morning TV news and the newspapers. A picture of him embracing Sally was on the front page. Everything he felt for her was there for the world to see. Everything he hadn't wanted the fire department's higher-ups to know. Sally was being hailed as a hero, as she should be. His leadership hadn't gone unnoticed either, or the abilities of the other firefighters.

By the time shift change came around, Ross was anxious to get out of the station. He wanted to see Sally, hold her and reassure himself that she was really okay. He'd called the hospital a couple of times to check on her after they had arrived back at the house. On the last call he'd been told she'd gone home. She would be with Kody.

Ross drove straight to Sally's house from the station. He all but ran to her door. Once again he hesitated there. Would she want to see him? What would he do if she didn't? Beg. Yes, beg was the plan. Somehow, he had to get through to her. He took his courage in hand and knocked. She didn't answer. He tried again. Nothing. He tried calling her on the phone and there was no answer. Slowly he walked back to his truck. Where was she?

Maybe she was at Kody's. He tried phoning him. There was no answer. He went by Kody's house. He wasn't home either. Where were they? Could they be at the station picking up Sally's car? Ross made a circle back by there. Sally's car was gone. He tried her phone. Still no answer.

He'd just have to go home and keep calling. After he saw to the horses, he'd put on his best shirt and pants, buy some flowers and chocolate, and try again. Fear gripped him. Was she nowhere to be found because she didn't want to see him?

Sally hoped what she thought she'd heard Ross say at the hospital was true. That he loved her. Maybe she'd just imagined it because she wanted his love so desperately. She loved him with all her heart. She was admitting it by coming out to his place unannounced.

He had acted as if he'd been relieved, as if she was his world and he'd gotten it back when she'd come up out of the drain. She was afraid that he was going to lose it again with the Battalion Chief standing right there. Ross hadn't seemed to care. It had been wonderful being in Ross's arms again. Having him hold her always made things better.

She glanced at the letter that lay on the swing next to her. It might not solve all their problems, but it might help.

Her heart picked up its pace when she saw Ross's truck coming down the drive. She went down the steps to meet him. Would he be mad or happy to see her?

He pulled the truck to a jerking stop, hopped out and ran to her. "I've been looking everywhere for you." He stopped just short of pulling her into his arms.

"I told Kody to let you know I was coming out here."

"He didn't, but then, he was probably punishing me for being such a jerk," he all but growled.

She shrugged. "You could be right."

Ross studied her for a few moments. "Are you okay? Really okay?"

The concern in his voice touched her heart. Why didn't he touch her? "I'm fine. Really. I just don't want to have to do anything like that again."

"I don't want you to have to either. It almost killed us both." His gaze held hers. "I would've died if you had. I love you."

"You do?"

"I do with all my heart." The intensity of his voice filled her with joy. "You might not have seen much evidence of it lately, but I do."

"I had hoped what I'd heard at the hospital was true."

Ross stepped closer, almost touching her chest with his. "Does that mean I have a chance? To straighten up, strive to be worthy of you? I don't care about promotions anymore, if I can't have you. I can go to a smaller fire department and work. But I won't live without you. I can't."

She placed her hand on his chest. "You're my hero. You've always been worthy enough. I've never doubted that I could trust you, or that you would protect me or be there if I needed someone. Even if we were just friends. But to have your love is so much more."

Ross scooped her into his arms and kissed her as if he would never let her go. She wrapped her arms around his neck and returned his kisses with equal devotion.

When he set her on her feet again, he looked into her eyes. "I love you, Sweet Sally. I will always."

Sally cupped his face with her hand. "And I love you with all my heart."

He kissed her so tenderly that she was afraid she would cry.

"May I show you just how much I love you?" Ross took her hands.

"I thought you'd never ask."

He led her up the steps and into the house.

Ross lay with Sally snuggled beside him. There had been days he'd thought he would never have this again. And never again would he take moments like this for granted. They were too precious. Life was too precious. What mattered was he and Sally being together.

"Hey, handsome. What're you thinking up there?" Sally looked at him from where her head rested on his chest.

"I was thinking what a lucky man I am."

"That was a nice answer." Her fingers trailed over his skin. "I consider myself pretty lucky too. Oh, that reminds me." She hopped out of bed and pulled on his firehouse T-shirt.

Ross watched as her beautiful body with its back marred by long scratches left the room. He winced. They were a reminder of what could have been. He heard the front door open. "Hey, where're you going?"

"I'll be right back. I have something to show you."

Seconds later the door opened again. Sally came into the room with an envelope in her hand.

"What do you have?"

She sat beside him. "This came in the mail yesterday. I didn't get it until I got home today. You were the first person I thought of sharing it with."

"What is it?"

"My MCAT score."

He sat straighter. "How did you do?"

She grinned at him. "Well enough to get into any medical school I want."

Ross gave a whoop and hugged her to him. "That's my Sweet Sally." He gave her a kiss.

"So, where're you thinking of going?" Could he stand it if she went far off? No, anywhere she went there would be a fire department. He'd just have to follow.

"I was thinking of staying here and going to Austin Medical. Kody has a doctor friend who could probably help me get a job afterward."

"Now, that sounds like a good plan. I'm so proud of you." He hugged her.

She met his gaze. "You know, it means a lot to me to have you in my corner."

Ross took her hand and kissed her palm. "You can always count on that."

"I've been thinking that now I know I'm going to medical school soon that maybe I should transfer to another station or maybe go to a private company."

He shook his head. "You don't have to do that. I won't ask you to."

She cupped his cheek. "You're not asking. Or demanding. If that's what it takes to help you, then I'm willing to do it. What matters most to me will always be you."

His heart swelled with love. "And you'll always come first with me."

"I love you, Ross."

His lips brushed hers. "And I love you."

EPILOGUE

THREE DAYS LATER Ross was about to walk out the door of the station when he got a call from Chief Marks. He wanted Ross to come by his office and see him that afternoon. Ross hesitated. He and Sally had plans to celebrate her medical school acceptance with Kody and Lucy that evening. She was cooking dinner for them at his place.

He grinned. It was his and Sally's place now. He loved knowing she would be there when he came home.

"Can we do it right now? I've plans this evening."

"Sure, come on over," said Chief Marks.

A short drive later, as Ross entered the office Chief Marks stood. "I hear you had an exciting shift the other night?"

"Yeah, the house did."

"You know, most firefighters go an entire

278 FIREFIGHTER'S UNEXPECTED FLING

career and are never involved in a child rescue like that."

"I know." Where was he going with this? It could have all been said over the phone.

Chief Marks's look turned serious. "I also heard the paramedic did an outstanding job as well."

"Yes, Sally was amazing."

"She's the one, isn't she?" The Chief watched him closely.

Ross sat straighter in his chair. "Yes, sir, she is. She's also the one for me. I plan to marry her if she'll have me. I appreciate all you've done for me but if I have to choose between the promotion or her I'm always going to pick her."

Battalion Chief Marks smiled. "I don't think you'll have to do that. The Chief was very impressed with the reports he received about the rescue. Some of it wasn't by the regulations but the end result was excellent. The boy will make a complete recovery. The decision on the new Battalion Chief had pretty much been made, but your leadership during the rescue sealed the deal. The Chief gave me the honor of telling you myself. You'll be our newest and youngest ever Battalion Chief." He stood and offered his hand. "Congratulations. You earned it."

With a huge grin, Ross took his hand. "Thank you, sir."

"The Chief plans to announce it when you, your house and the paramedic, uh, Sally, are awarded a citation in a couple of weeks. But he wanted you to know about it now."

Ross left the Chief's office feeling on top of the world. He wouldn't ruin Sally's celebration of her success tonight. It should be all about her. Instead he would tell her his news while they were alone later in bed so they could have their own special celebration.

He touched his injured shoulder. Life was good. Especially now that he had Sally in it.

Sally was at her apartment with Lucy, packing up the last of the small things to take to Ross's. It hadn't required much persuasion on his part to get her to agree to move to the ranch. She loved it there. Almost as much as she loved him. The last few weeks had been a whirlwind. Between her acceptance to medical school, Ross getting his promotion to Battalion Chief and them both receiving citations from the mayor for their work saving the boy, her life and heart were full.

Tomorrow, after Ross and Kody's shift ended they and a few of the other station members would load up the furniture she wanted to keep and move it out to the ranch. One of the firefighters at the station was moving into her apartment and taking over the lease.

"Here, Aunt Sally." Lucy handed her an empty box she'd sent her after.

"Thanks. I think this should almost get it." Sally pulled a stack of books off a shelf in her living room.

The flash of red lights through the window and the sound of a large engine that she knew well drew her attention. What was going on? Was an apartment burning? Someone hurt? She hadn't heard a siren. But they usually turned them off when they entered a neighborhood.

"What's happening?" Lucy asked.

"I don't know but whatever it is the firefighters will take care of it, I'm sure."

The roar of the heavy truck sounded near as if it had pulled to a stop in front of her building.

The emergency lights coming in from the windows reflected around the blank walls of the apartment. Sally hurried to the door. Lucy was at her heels. She opened the door to find the large red engine parked in front of her building. In the near darkness, the lights flashing made a real show.

Ross climbed out of the front passenger seat. He was wearing his usual firehouse uniform. This was his last shift before he started his new job, which would require a white shirt and black pants.

Sally walked toward him. "What's wrong? What're y'all doing here?"

Lucy ran past her. "Daddy!"

She looked beyond Ross to see Kody's truck parked behind the engine. The other firefighters on the shift stood by the engine with smiles on their faces.

"Ross, what's going on?" Sally asked.

He came to stand in front of her. "As my last official act as Captain at Station Twelve, I ordered this crew of firefighters to bring me here to ask you something."

She looked at the men at the truck, including her brother, whose smile had broadened, and his daughter, then around at her neighbors, who had come out of their apartments to see what was going on. "You couldn't have done it over the phone?"

He shook his head. "This isn't the kind of question you should ask over the phone."

Sally started to tremble. Her gaze met his.

Ross took her hand and went down on one knee.

Her heart beat wildly.

"Sally Davis, will you marry me?"

Her eyes filled with moisture, making Ross's handsome face blurry. She blinked. Nodding, she said, "Yes."

With a whoop, Ross came onto both feet and grabbed her, twirling her around.

There was clapping and cheers from those around them.

Ross set her feet on the ground before he gave her a kiss so tender she almost started tearing up again.

She looked at him with all the love she felt. "You know, Battalion Chief Lawson, I think Dr. Sally Lawson will sound perfect."

Ross smiled. "As long as we're together, life will be perfect for me."

Sally came up on her toes and kissed him. "For me too."

* * * * *

LET'S TALK

Romance

For exclusive extracts, competitions
and special offers, find us online:

- facebook.com/millsandboon
- @millsandboonuk
- @millsandboon

Or get in touch on 0844 844 1351*

For all the latest titles coming soon,
visit millsandboon.co.uk/nextmonth